a dangerous woman

DEBRA LEE

D0125890

W◍RLDWIDE®

TORONTO • NEW YORK • LONDON
AMSTERDAM • PARIS • SYDNEY • HAMBURG
STOCKHOLM • ATHENS • TOKYO • MILAN
MADRID • WARSAW • BUDAPEST • AUCKLAND

*To my mother and father who gave me life. To my
husband and sons for sharing a home with a writer.*

*To my very good friend Kathy, who was gracious enough
to read first drafts of most of my work.*

Recycling programs
for this product may
not exist in your area.

A DANGEROUS WOMAN

A Worldwide Mystery/October 2009

First published by SynergEbooks.

ISBN-13: 978-0-373-26688-3

Printed in U.S.A.

ONE

HAD I KNOWN PEOPLE I have feelings for were going to start turning up dead, I doubt I would have been so critical of the day. As it turned out, I was unaware of the horrors that awaited me. So the complaining began.

April showers bring May flowers. I would like to add to that catchy phrase, if they don't drown first. The monstrous clouds over central Pennsylvania threatened to hang steady until the last drop of moisture was squeezed from each one. This created growing irritability and restlessness in man and beast.

To prove my point, the Fergusons' terrier got a taste of blood after sinking razor-sharp, petite fangs into my wrist instead of the newspaper I slipped inside the screen door. As I rounded the corner of Front Street and Broadway, the big black tomcat that prowls outside the video store growled and hissed at me from his hunched position beneath a leaky awning.

So as it rained cats and dogs, I, Fay Cunningham, publisher of The Susquehanna Valley Daily, questioned my decision to make a second major lifestyle change within the last year.

"A few more blocks and all second thoughts about my decision will disappear," I repeated to myself as I flung rolled newspapers onto porches.

Yes, indeed. Once I climb the steps to Joe Wise's rundown mansion that stands on the upper side of Broadway, and am invited inside for the routine afternoon tea and conversation, all negative thoughts will be chased away by this self-made millionaire's words of wisdom.

The fifteen minutes it took me to reach Joe's front porch had made my need to see him more urgent. Besides suffering from a growing state of depression and a powerful craving for a meal loaded with fat, I was wet and chilled to the bone. I dropped my umbrella and watched it skip across the concrete floor as I hurried toward the closed door that should have been flung open by now.

The ancient door knocker received a ferocious work out from me before I heard footsteps in the foyer. A complete minute must have passed before I could respond to the live Barbie doll who opened the door a crack to say, "Yes, can I help you?"

Stammering, "Yes…Joe. Is he here?"

"Mr. Wise is napping," I was told, and watched the door close completely before my temporary state of surprise passed and I gave the door knocker another rap.

The door creaked open a few inches, while doll-eyes glared down at me. "Is there something else?"

My eyes seemed unable to leave hers as I slipped a newspaper through the crack.

"Joe's paper."

Her thanks was barely audible as she latched on to the rolled newspaper before the door slid shut, with the sound of the key turning in the lock immediately afterward.

I have no idea how many seconds I stood, dazed and confused, before I picked up my umbrella and reluctantly left Joe Wise's property.

I arrived at the local gossip corner a half hour earlier than usual. Too early for the mid-afternoon regulars. The edge of town restaurant's L-shaped parking lot was almost vacant. My gas guzzling Lincoln was right where I left it nearly two hours ago. It was an unwelcome surprise to see Mitch Malone's economically efficient dwarf-sized pickup truck parked alongside my car.

I wasn't in the mood to see the fit-as-a-fiddle

former police chief. The truth is, I didn't want him to see me temporarily ease my depression with a smorgasbord of unhealthy food. I wanted to indulge and enjoy, without hearing him remind me of how I was defeating the purpose of my "on foot" paper route. Then I'd have to remind him, my decision to do the route was not just to knock off the forty pounds I gained after quitting my twenty-year, pack-a-day, nicotine addiction. I also wanted to open the lines of communication with my customers. Hear firsthand, compliments, suggestions, and complaints about the newspaper I publish.

THE BELL OVER the restaurant's door announced my entrance. I got a pleasant whiff of cigarette smoke and fat frying as I watched Willie zip out of the kitchen and go directly to the coffee machine the instant she saw me. "It's gettin' pretty wicked lookin'," she said in reference to the coffee.

"How 'bout I just make a fresh pot," she offered after giving me a closer look.

"Don't bother. I need a shot of something stiff."

Willie chuckled as she went ahead and filled a mug with the scorched black brew. I waited until she started around the counter before heading to the end booth where Mitch was seated. His nose remained in the newspaper he had spread out in front of him when I slid into the seat across from him.

Willie put my mug of coffee down on the center of the newspaper. I'm certain she did this to antagonize Mitch. It didn't appear to faze him though. He went right on reading.

"I'll have your salad in a jiffy," she told me, and started to take off again. That is, until my words stopped her in her tracks.

"Make it a burger, fries, and super thick chocolate shake."

Mitch's fascination with the agricultural section of the newspaper halted. I didn't have to look. I could feel his eyes glaring at me.

"Must a been one heck of a day."

I waited until I heard Willie shift into high gear again and head for the kitchen before responding.

"I've had better."

"Suppose old man Wise was too busy gloatin' to pay you any attention."

"Gloating?"

"You shouldn't let that man's actions get to you, Fay."

I don't know if my face was beginning to tingle from anger or confusion. Perhaps a combination of both. It was my anger I acted on when I called back toward the kitchen.

"Hey, Willie, add a hot fudge sundae to my order."

"You're only hurting yourself, you know."

His comment managed to put me on the brink of tears. I knew if I couldn't stop them, it would prove another victory for the reformed Mitchell Malone. Of late, the man was beginning to become my biggest daily irritant with his purified lifestyle and arrogant attitude. It was days like this one, I missed the former chain-smoking, overweight, foul-mouthed alcoholic he once was.

I am not certain just how I pulled it off, but I stiffened my spine, blinked back the tears, and was about to tell him what he could do with his advice when he started again. Only this time, he was back to attacking Joe Wise.

"It wouldn't surprise me if he wasn't on the phone plannin' the biggest bash of his life."

"You still like it rare, I hope?" Willie said, as she put the plate of food in front of me.

I looked directly over into Mitch's eyes when I responded. "A little blood in the diet's good for what ails me."

Willie giggled.

Mitch didn't find my statement amusing. His

way of letting me know it was to fold up his news-paper, pick up his Stetson from the seat next to him, plop it down on the graying waves on top of his head, and start scooting out of the booth.

It was at that moment, I knew we were even for the day. The perfect time to part company. But I couldn't allow it. At least not until he explained his comments about my dear friend, Joe Wise.

"If I don't eat this plate of lard, will you tell me why Joe was supposed to be higher than a kite today?"

He took nearly a full minute of sitting on the edge of his seat contemplating his decision. Actually, he was pouting. In the meantime, my food was cooling down fast. When he slid his cowboy-clad feet back under the tabletop and looked my way, I knew he decided to stay.

"Joe didn't tell you?"

"Tell me what?"

"His lifelong nemesis turned up dead this morn-ing."

TWO

SILENCE. I COULD NOT speak. My brain shut down on me. I was unable to move. My breath felt blocked. In what had to have been only seconds, in which I sat with such limited abilities, I was able to see. Those doll-eyes were once again glaring down at me, drawing me into the inner depths of their skinny young owner.

What I saw there jolted me so severely that when my body jumped, so did my arm, banging into my plate. Food scattered everywhere.

"Didn't think you even knew the old playboy," Mitch said, as he picked up french fries and tossed them back onto the plate.

"He gave me my start in business."

"Thought Joe—"

"Joe stepped in when his brother tried to take over the newspaper without my knowledge."

Mitch stopped picking up french fries and was glaring at me again. "What?"

"You could be a suspect in his murder."

"Thomas was murdered?"

"Callin' it an accidental drownin' so far. I'm not convinced the old guy slipped under the bathwater without some help."

When Mitch picked up a french fry and held it between his formerly nicotine stained fingers like he would a cigarette, I knew he was genuinely concerned. But was that concern out of fear his police buddies would treat Thomas Wise's death as an accident and close the case without investigating the possibility of foul play? Or was he worried they would conclude it was murder and place me on the top of their list of suspects?

INSTEAD OF questioning him about it, I decided to give him something else to think about.

"I didn't see Joe today. According to the young blonde waif who answered his door, Joe was napping."

I looked straight over into midnight blue eyes, which was like seeing a reflection of my own.

"Joe doesn't nap," I pointed out. "At least not when he knows I'm due to arrive."

I assumed Mitch would immediately want to know if I knew the woman. But no, white teeth sparkled between silver beard and mustache. He was snickering like he did before one of his judgmental comments.

"Thought you licked that streak of jealousy, Fay? You know it'll only give you—"

"Gray hair and wrinkles like you?"

The purpose of my insult was to shut him up. Certainly not to create the burst of laughter that came from him.

If the restaurant hadn't started filling with customers, I know I would have dumped my plate of food over his head. Instead, I took a deep breath, shoved back my shoulders, and left the restaurant.

Go ahead and laugh, I thought, because I would have the last laugh once the annoying man realized I stuck him paying the bill for the third time in the past week.

THREE

THE RAIN HAD EASED to a drizzle. Any amount was too much, as far as I was concerned.

I slid in behind the wheel of my older model luxury car. My eyes instantly zeroed in on the glove compartment, while my mind was telling them to look away. Turn away. Turn off the fierce urge to open that compartment and reach for them. They're probably staler than this dreadful weather anyway, an inner voice reminded.

The pack of cigarettes had been in my glove compartment for months. I bought them the day Allen told me he wanted a divorce. I would like to believe it was sheer willpower that kept me from breaking the seal on that green and white pack of smokes that day, but that would be only half true. Mitch's words of encouragement kept me strong enough to fight off the powerful urge for a blast of nicotine to my system.

On this particular day, it was because of him, my

skin crawled in need of a fix. I closed my eyes, latched on to the steering wheel, and ordered myself to take three deep, relaxing breaths. I took five before slowly opening my eyes. My mouth widened into a smile as I took a long look at myself in the rear-view mirror. This time, I did it my way, and more important, on my own.

"Take that, Mitchell Malone," I said to my glowing reflection.

I pulled out of the parking lot and headed back toward town. Joe should be awake from his nap. If he's not, I'll wake him. Miss Barbie Doll will step aside or get shoved aside. This old gal wasn't taking a backseat to any more pretty young Twiggys. Once was enough in Fay Cunningham's lifetime.

"I'm in love with her, Fay," Allen had confessed that mournful day months ago as he pranced around our bedroom like a caged wild animal. I was sitting on the edge of our king-sized bed, a stack of wet balled up tissues next to me. If only I could stop whimpering, I told myself. Then I might feel more than the heartrending pain that numbed my other emotions. Anger, for one. I wished I could get mad enough to throw something at the man I had given the last twenty-five years of my life to.

Weeks went by though before the numbness slid

away and made room for the onslaught of every-thing else. The loneliness, fear, and anger, all took a shot at me over the days that followed my signing the divorce papers my husband took upon himself to hand deliver to me. I got the house, and the out-rageous mortgage payment. Of course, Allen agreed to finish paying for our daughter, Alicia's, college education. Three years to go and he was off the hook. I agreed to keep my fingers out of his law firm earnings so long as he kept his paws out of those from my newspaper business. I also got Kitty, our indoor Calico cat. Allen got Dana, his model thin twenty-something paralegal.

As my car coasted along Broadway, well below the posted twenty-five miles per hour speed limit, I felt some of the gusto from minutes before begin to seep away. I had Mitch to thank for it, too. Maybe he was right. Was it jealousy I felt when it was a beautiful young woman who greeted me instead of Joe? Had I become jealous of all women younger, thinner and prettier than me? Or just the ones who entered my turf?

Joe was my turf. Twenty years ago when my parents retired to Arizona, Joe Wise was appointed my Godfather. To be completely accurate, Joseph Costello was named my Godfather, the name Joe

Wise went by before he left his home in Italy to come to America. In Joe's words, his brother, Thomas suggested they change their last name to Wise. The brothers would become the Wise men. Joe never told me the whole story behind the name change.

I was already married five years by the time Joe became my Godfather, but Father insisted I needed more than Allen to look after me. At the time, I was furious. Now when I look back, I have to admit that my father knew what he was doing.

In the beginning, I resented Joe's interference in my life. Enough so that I went to his biggest rival, his brother Thomas, to secure a loan to start my newspaper business. When Thomas discovered I had me a little gold mine, he wanted it all for himself. Joe to the rescue of this damsel in distress. I am forever grateful.

I turned my car onto Popular Avenue and made a sharp left onto the narrow paved road. About a hundred yards in, I made a uey before taking the right onto the rear of Joe's property, where I left my car. There are four entrances into the three story brick castle-shaped home.

After knocking, waiting, and unsuccessfully trying to open each of the four locked doors, I gave up.

A steady rain was beating down on me by this time. My shoulders were up around my ears as I dashed for the shelter of my car. Ducking inside, I was looking straight over at Joe's garage. My curiosity would not permit me to leave without checking to see if Joe's old Mercedes was parked inside. This knowledge caused a few unpleasant words to skip through my head.

I dashed around the front of my car. My sneakers landed on the pile of wet leaves at the precise moment I saw them. Too late to avoid the slipping and sliding. I did manage to get my balance a second before my legs did a complete split. This time those same unpleasant words, and several more, did more than skip through my head.

It would have been easy to let a few more fly out of my mouth after peeking through a dirty garage window and seeing two empty parking stalls. I didn't have my car backed all the way out of Joe's driveway when it dawned on me where he probably was. Every Wednesday, without fail, he drives across the river to the Farmer's Market to snatch up the end of the day specials. It was Wednesday, and the end of the market's day. And it took getting soaked down to my undergarments and over-stretched inner thigh muscles for that to occur to me.

I glanced up at my reflection long enough to give myself a much needed pep talk. "Look at it this way, old gal, the day can't possibly get any worse. Or can it?"

FOUR

BY THE TIME I APPROACHED my driveway, I was actually beginning to see myself curled up in front of the fireplace with a book, after a long, relaxing soak in the tub. A pleasant evening awaited me. Or would have if Mitch Malone's pickup wasn't parked in my driveway.

I was about to shift into Reverse and drive off, but it was too late. Mitch spotted me, because he was already getting out of his truck. It crossed my mind to drive into the garage and hit the Remote button to close the door before he had time to dart underneath. I probably would have done just that, had I not glanced in the rear-view mirror once I was inside the garage. When I saw him reach into the passenger's side of his truck for something, as usual, curiosity got the best of me. Once I saw what looked like a pizza box, I decided against shutting him outside.

"I come offerin' peace" I was told as I stepped

out of my car and was handed the pizza box in exchange for the key to my house.

The perfect gentleman held the door for me before following my lead into the kitchen.

I put the box on the table. Mitch dropped my keys down next to it, then broke into the silence that stretched so tightly between us.

"It's extra pepperoni."

I finally looked over at him and cracked a smile.

"You really do feel guilty, don't you?"

"For what?"

I wasn't in the mood to explain in detail what a nagging pain in the butt he had become lately. Actually, I didn't owe him an explanation of any kind. For supposedly being such an intelligent man, he could be so thick sometimes, especially when it came to understanding me. Or women in general.

Mitch filled two glasses with bottled spring water while I dug in the cupboard for paper plates. Before I joined him at the table, I grabbed a bottle of soda from the refrigerator. He was staring at me. I could feel it as I twisted off the bottle cap and took a long swallow. It wasn't until he went to the refrigerator and got his own soda that I looked over at him, completely bewildered.

"I do understand." He took a swallow of his soda, then added, "I'm sorry, okay?"

Even if I could have spoken, I wasn't sure what I'd say. One thing was certain though, the man was an absolute wonder.

"You know, Fay, I'd do about anything for you. Except, if you ask me to share a cigarette with you, I'd have to refuse it."

"Of course you would. And I'd want you to. But I really don't know why we're even discussing this. I have no desire to light up one of those stinky things."

I was dying for one. I'm sure Mitch knew it, too. But the subject was dropped and we polished off the pizza in peace.

It wasn't until we had worked our way into the living room and Mitch was building a fire, while I made myself comfortable on the couch, that he finally asked me about the woman who answered Joe's door earlier in the day.

"I haven't a clue who she is," I told him.

"What about a daughter? Maybe a niece or—"

"No. Joe doesn't have any family left. At least not now that Thomas is gone."

If I hadn't reminded him about Joe's brother, possibly a victim of murder, I believe Mitch would have eased down next to me. The man may have given up his badge to become an organic farmer, but the need for truth and justice continued to walk within him. I knew his gut instinct was telling him Thomas's death might not be accidental, and he would sniff around like a bloodhound until he satisfied himself with the truth.

"You mind if I stop by a little later?"

"Only if you promise to tell me everything you find out."

He leaned over and planted a kiss on my forehead. When he straightened, I could tell by the way he narrowed his eyes and smiled that he understood it was pointless to deny knowing what I was talking about.

"You'll know everything I do."

He left himself out, while I remained in a corner of the couch with my feet tucked up underneath me. It would have been so easy to remain in that position, gazing into the snapping and cracking flames before me, my mind nowhere in particular. But besides having the curiosity of a cat, I also have a strong sense of responsibility. It might be going overboard to make another trip to Joe's home, but a telephone call was an absolute must.

I pressed the memory button and number five on my cordless phone and listened to three rings.

"Hello. The Wise residence."

It was her. I recognized the flat voice immediately. It was the waif from earlier. Who was she? And what was she doing answering Joe's telephone? Why had she answered his door?

"Put Joe on the phone, please."

"I'm sorry, Mr. Wise can't come to the phone right now."

"Why not?"

"Mr. Wise is having his bath…"

Whatever else she said went unheard when I dropped the phone and shot off the couch.

FIVE

THE MINUTE SHE SAID Joe was taking a bath, the
alarms began going off inside me. It wasn't the fact
that Joe always bathed right before breakfast that set
off those alarms. It was remembering what Mitch
said earlier about Thomas possibly having help
sliding under the bathwater that had me breaking
speed limits to get to Joe's place.

I felt pending danger the instant I laid eyes on
that sweet-looking skinny woman. It was not sweet-
ness I saw when I looked into those glossy eyes of
hers, though. It was what I didn't see inside that
gave me so much fright.

The rational side of me attempted to warn that I
was jumping to the wrong conclusion. But the other
side knew there were people without souls. People
like the ones I ran a newspaper story about a few
months back. Unscrupulous individuals who prey
on the elderly. Those brilliant scam artists who can
con a senior out of everything they own without a

second thought about the devastation left behind by their crime. In the worse case scenario, the senior is not only taken for everything it took a lifetime to acquire, but their lives have been taken as well.

That thought is why I stepped on the gas.

THE RAIN HAD finally stopped, but a blinding fog was settling in right behind it. Joe's house appeared dark except for the yellow glow coming from the back porch light.

I stepped out of my car and headed toward the light. The sound of a twig snapped somewhere behind me. I refused the urge to look over my shoulder, but picked up speed until my sneakers landed on the paint blistered porch floor. I felt safer in the glow of the porch light and slowly peeked over my shoulder. When a pair of eyes flashed through the haze from a tree branch, I dashed for the door, rattling the knob and banging on the glass top.

The kitchen light came on, but I didn't let up my attack on the door. I heard the deadbolt slide over and turned the knob and pushed. I was greeted by her. The emotionless creature I already decided I did not like.

Before she had a chance to protest my intrusion, I made my first demand.

"Where is Joe?"

"Mr. Wise is not here."

"I'll just check that out for myself," I told her as I brushed against the silky sleeve of her nightgown.

The entire time I went from room to room, lighting up the house like a Christmas tree, I was calling out Joe's name. The search took several minutes to complete. In the end, I hadn't found Joe.

I was halfway down the open staircase when Miss Frosty appeared in the foyer.

"I told you Mr. Wise wasn't here," I was reminded in a tone that made my flesh crawl.

"Who are you anyway?"

"Angel Adams." *Angels don't have killer eyes.* "I'm Mr. Wise's housekeeper."

"What happened to Ethel?"

"Ethel?"

I was too frustrated to explain to this stranger that Ethel had been Joe's housekeeper and companion for longer than I could remember. I breezed past her and headed back toward the kitchen. At the back door I stopped, looked over my shoulder, and made direct eye contact with her. "You be sure to tell Mr. Wise Fay Cunningham was here," I said.

Her eyes followed me out the door and off the porch into the fog. I felt them. As much as I wanted to make a mad dash for my car, I did not do it. Instead, I stood tall and bravely marched onward. That is until an owl gave out a chilling screech that put me in my car in two giant leaps.

The drive home was a nightmare. If it had not been for the lines down the center of the road and along the edge, I would not have known where the road began or ended. I drove at a snail's pace, hoping-praying, for a set of taillights to follow. No taillights miraculously appeared. But I did spot a reflector on a mailbox, alerting me the road to my place was just ahead. For the life of me though, I could not find it in the haunting fog. Out of nowhere, a pair of headlights shot at me from behind, blinding my vision even more.

It was impossible to slow down anymore without coming to a complete stop. I was too afraid to increase the car's speed. So I coasted toward the berm, holding my breath a drainage ditch wasn't there. I finally got lucky. My Lincoln didn't take a nose dive. I also managed to bring the car to a stop without hitting anything or being rear-ended.

Once the blinding headlights shot out around me, I wheeled back onto the road and made a uey. With that successfully accomplished, I flipped on the air vent to blow dry the perspiration that was beading up at various spots on my face.

Calm. Remain calm. Breathe deeply. You'll get there. So how come I doubted the voice that was whispering inside my head? Suddenly headlights gave me another blast from behind. I had no way of knowing if it was the same vehicle from minutes before, but I had a hunch it was.

Don't panic. Stay calm. Don't let your imagination run wild. Then came, don't slow to a stop again. Hit the gas and get this buggy moving. Which is exactly what I did. I was moving, and so was the vehicle behind me.

Adrenaline rushed through me, zapping at my nerve endings and pounding into my flesh. When the driver behind me flicked his lights on high, a second after being blinded by the flash, I caught sight of the road sign. The turn off to my home was upon me. I whipped the steering wheel to the right. My foot came off the accelerator a split second before I went into a spin.

Somehow, I managed to steady the wheel and straighten out the car. It was impossible to level out my breathing until I saw the lights were gone.

Whoever was following me hadn't made the turn. This did enable me to breathe a slight bit easier. But I did not let down my guard as I crept along until I spotted the reflector on my own mailbox.

SIX

RAW NERVES REMAINED with me as I rooted around in a kitchen cupboard. When I found the bottle of brandy, I didn't waste time filling a glass. I drank straight from the bottle. A few large swallows came before I allowed myself to sip and enjoy the pleasant taste and warm feeling as it entered my system.

My nerves were still a bit jumpy when I left the bottle on the counter and headed upstairs, assuring myself a long soak in the tub would bring total calm. While water ran into the tub, I went through three bedrooms, flipping on lights, checking under beds, and inside closets. This is not part of my evening routine. But then, my evenings aren't typically so traumatic.

By the time I slid beneath bubbles, I can honestly say I felt safe. Or safer.

I rolled my head from side to side until I located a comfortable position to rest it in. My eyes closed. I told myself to let go completely. Clear your head of all worrisome thoughts. I was doing it, too.

First, my left hand slid down porcelain and sank into the soothing warmth. My right fingers willingly lost their grip and made the plunge as well, instantly sending me into an upright position from the stinging sensation that pricked my wrist.

I took a close look at the flesh wounds the Ferguson dog's spiked teeth had caused. The skin around the miniature puncture wounds was red and swollen, but there were no streaks running up the inside of my arm. Whatever that meant. I vaguely remembered hearing somewhere those streaks under the skin are dangerous. But was it because infection was setting in or blood poisoning? I thought the latter was it. If someone happened to stick you with a lead pencil, watch for the streaks.

It didn't really matter. The way the day had gone, the little beast probably had rabies. I'd have to remember to check with the Fergusons to be sure their little pooch had his shots. It probably wouldn't hurt to start carrying a pocketful of dog biscuits on my daily route, either.

Tomorrow would be soon enough to take care of things like that, I decided. It was relaxation time. Certainly not the time and place to give my mind a workout. I didn't want to overload the circuitry and risk a short that would result in frying myself in the bathtub.

I was finally becoming comfortable. My over-stretched inner thigh muscles even felt like they were easing back into their proper place. Life was okay again. At least at that very moment it was. My brain waves were slowing down, coming close to shutting down. The tranquility was divine. I was so light, so….

Something squeaked. A door. My eyelids flipped open. Then it was a creak.

Something, someone, was in my house. In my bedroom. My heart was in my throat. My rear froze fast to the tub, while I strained my ears to hear it again. When I didn't, enough time had passed for me to consider who might have invaded the privacy of my home. I called out Mitch's name several times before it occurred to me Mitch couldn't be in my house. The doors were locked. Mitch didn't have a key yet.

My brain was spinning into high gear again. *Don't just sit there like a sitting duck. Get yourself up and out of there,* this voice inside my head ordered. Which is exactly what I was attempting to do when the bathroom door swung open.

I screamed. Kitty's hair shot out like a porcupine as she hissed and sprang back into the bedroom.

Several seconds passed before I lost the death grip on the side of the tub and was able to breathe again. Once my vital signs returned to normal, I quickly dried myself and pulled on a baggy sweatsuit. Then it was time to make amends to the cat.

The one sure way to do this was to open a can of cat food. Nothing, not even the fright I gave her, deterred Kitty from appearing to the sound of the electric can opener.

I assumed my apology was not fully acceptable when Kitty finished eating and refused to join me in the living room. The fire needed wood and a few stabs with the poker before I settled down on the couch. Temptation was high to pick up the telephone and call Joe's place again. But it was getting late. If Joe had returned home, he surely would be in bed. His internal clock was set with the early to bed early to rise alarm. But then, it didn't appear he was having a typical day either.

That being the case, I did call. I let it ring at least a dozen times before I hung up. Worry consumed me all over again. I looked at the grandfather clock in the corner. It was ten o'clock already. Where was Joe? Where was Mitch?

Mitch did say he'd be dropping by later. So where was he? I tapped out Mitch's numbers and got his answering machine. I didn't wait for the beep to leave my message. I didn't have a message.

After getting up and pacing around the room several times, I returned to the kitchen to make a second attempt at getting Kitty to join me in the living room. She refused, of course. Back in the living room, I pushed back a corner of the drape to have a look outside. I faced a wall of fog.

I finally selected a book from one of the two floor-to-ceiling bookshelves and carried it back to the couch with me. Once I convinced myself to concentrate on the meaning of the words I read, I was able to be transported into a world gone by.

SEVEN

THE SOUND OF THE DOORBELL woke me. More like
startled me into wakefulness. It took me a few
moments to figure out where I was and what had
shaken me from dreamland. Or more correctly, the
land of nightmares.

"I'm coming. I'm coming," I shouted, and
pushed myself off the couch, book tumbling from
my lap when I stood.

It was breaking daylight when I yanked the door
open and looked up into Mitch's weary eyes.

"Need some coffee badly" was his greeting as he
stepped inside and headed straight for the kitchen.
By the looks of him he needed a shower and some
sleep a lot more.

"What's happened?" I barely had the question
out when one of my nightmares flashed before me.

"Joe... Oh God, tell me nothing's happened to
Joe."

When Mitch picked the bottle of brandy off the

counter from where I left it the night before, I feared
the worst. Before he had the cap twisted off, he put
the bottle back down on the counter. I had no idea
what a struggle that decision really was for him.

"It's not Joe," he finally told me.

He seemed unable to face me and started filling
the coffee pot with water.

"Thomas. You found out he was murdered then?"

Mitch turned off the water and slowly tilted his
head in my direction. "It's Ethel, Fay."

"Joe's Ethel?"

"She was found a little after midnight. Bunch a
kids decided on a camp out after the rain stopped."
Mitch took a breather to pull out a table chair and
guide me into it. After pulling a chair up next to me
and folding himself into it, he proceeded. "They
were partyin' is what they were doin.' Sobered up
really quick when one a the girls opened the refrigerator."

"Refrigerator?"

"They were partyin' next to someone's dump site
in the woods."

When Mitch let go of my hand, I latched back
onto his. "Ethel was in the refrigerator?"

Mitch's eyes were bubbling up with tears. This
time when he pulled away, I let him. It was obvious

he needed a moment to get a grip on his emotions. Which he seemed to do by the time he filled two mugs and returned to the table with them.

"She was gagged and tied up, Fay. Looks like she was stuffed in there alive, too. She suffocated."

Everything he told me was too horrible to absorb all at once. I refused to let myself see the image of what Mitch actually had seen. I also refused to accept the fact that Mitch was talking about the Ethel Johnson I knew most of my adult life.

"How do you know for sure that it's Ethel? I mean, maybe someone that looks like—"

"It's her, Fay. Her sister identified the body."

Down deep, I knew what Mitch said was the truth. Ethel was the one found dead. But on the surface, I still could not believe it. And I certainly wasn't ready to accept it.

"Got to meet the pretty young thing you told me was at Joe's yesterday."

"Joe! Oh, God, how is he handling this? Is he—"

"Don't know. He wasn't home when I dropped by before comin' here."

"Wasn't home," I repeated in disbelief.

It didn't take long for the anger to begin cooking within me. Something was terribly wrong and that woman was to blame. I just knew it.

"So did Angel tell you where Joe is?"

"Said he left on a trip."

"A trip! That's ridiculous. Joe would have told me if he was going away. She's lying, Mitch."

"You say her name's Angel?"

"Angel Adams is what she told me. That's probably a lie too."

"You gonna be okay if I take off for a while?"

"No. This time you're taking me with you."

"I'm only goin' home to feed the animals."

"You really expect me to believe that?"

"It's the truth. I have no authority to investigate this case."

"As if that'll stop you."

"Don't you have a newspaper to run or somethin'?"

"I have papers to deliver this afternoon. But I still have my assistant in charge of the daily operations, remember?"

Mitch exhaled in defeat. "Okay, you can come with me, but I really do have to stop by the farm."

"I'll be changed before you have time to rinse our mugs," I assured.

I was in my jeans and sneakers in record time and raced back down the stairs and into the empty kitchen. The mugs had been rinsed and left on the counter to air dry. Mitch was gone though. At least he wasn't in the kitchen.

I dashed back into the hallway and to the front door. As I pulled it open, I got a glimpse of the rear-end of his pickup before it disappeared around the curve in the road.

Somehow, I stopped myself before I stamped my foot like a child on the verge of throwing a temper tantrum. I was no child. I was a full-grown woman. The publisher of a very successful newspaper business too. And that certainly wouldn't have been possible if I had made a habit of minding my own business.

It is not a crime to admit I've done my own share of sniffing out a story to make headlines. So looking around for information about Ethel's murder wouldn't be any different, I decided. And at the same time, I could track down the whereabouts of Joe, even if it meant choking the truth out of one Angel Adams.

By the time I left the house, I had convinced myself I could get to the bottom of things without the help of Mitch Malone. His disappearing act was proof enough he felt I'd be more of a hindrance than a help to his investigation. So I really didn't have any other choice than to go it alone.

EIGHT

I LEFT MY CAR PARKED on Broadway and hiked up the steep hill to the rear of Joe's property. If Miss Angel was lurking about, I didn't want her to see me coming. I wanted to take her by surprise like she did me the day before.

Before checking out the house, I decided to have a look inside the garage. I found two empty parking stalls. But that was no guarantee Angel Adams wasn't inside the house. And just because I knew most of Joe's neighbors, didn't mean one of them wouldn't find delight in calling the police to report a peeping Tom if I started peering in the house windows.

I took my chances anyway. Or perhaps, in hopes someone would call the police. At least they might be able to get the aloof Angel to 'fess up to the whereabouts of Joe.

There was no movement inside the house from

either of the two rear windows I looked through. While I was there, I thought I'd give the porch door a try. Locked. So were all the other doors I tried.

On the west side of the house, I noticed one of the windows had a screen in it. All I had to do was figure out how to climb up to it. I started looking around for something sturdy enough to stand on when I saw old man Mr. Anderson. He was pretending to be filling the bird-feeder in his front yard, but it was as plain as day he was watching me.

I surprised him, as intended, when I waved and called over a good morning. Then I proceeded in my search as if I had every right to be doing what I was doing.

The only thing I saw that looked tall enough for me to be able to reach the window, was a tin bucket I found on the back porch. *Let's hope it can withstand the weight of me,* crossed my mind as I positioned it under the window and stepped aboard. I managed to remove the screen without a hitch. It surprised and pleased me that I had enough upper body strength to pull myself up the wall of bricks and rest my fanny on the window ledge.

It was when I was maneuvering myself around so I could slip down inside that I felt it.

The backside of my jeans had caught on something. As I twisted around to try and free myself, the ripping sound was overshadowed by the bang of an upstairs door closing. A decision had to be made without delay. I got a quick glimpse of Mr. Anderson before he disappeared inside his house. I don't know if it was knowing he wouldn't see me running from the scene, or if the light footsteps on the stairs made up my mind to take a flying leap to the ground.

I missed the bucket all right, but my right foot landed in a chipmunk hole. I might have imagined the crunch I heard when my ankle turned sideways, but the excruciating pain I felt was real enough as I hobbled down the hill to my car.

YOU MESSED UP things real good this time, old gal, I told myself as I attempted to drive home. I had my lower body shifted to the right on my seat so I could use my left foot on the gas and brake pedals. I was having trouble believing the stupid stunt I had just pulled. Now how was I going to deliver papers? How was I going to shed pounds sitting on my fanny? And how was I going to track down Joe and find Ethel's killer?

My mind kept repeating Mitch's name in answer

to that last question. But I refused to listen. I'd find the answers without him. No sprained ankle was going to stand in the way of Fay Cunningham.

NINE

I HAD MY ANKLE PACKED in ice and propped up on the coffee table when I started making telephone calls. Doug, the energetic and bright young man I had running the business end of the paper for me, was called first. I explained my predicament to him. He had to find someone to temporarily take over my paper route. That was a piece-a-cake in comparison to the other problems he was trying to solve.

"We've got big trouble brewing with the editorial staff, Fay. Kate wants a larger column. Bill wants a raise and—"

"And I have complete faith in your dealing with all of them, Doug. So I'll just say good-bye so you can get to it."

I hung up before he could protest. I also hoped it would remind him of our agreement. The day my divorce to Allen was finalized, I took a good look at myself in the mirror; at the person I had become. I saw very little I liked there. The middle-aged, overweight person that looked back at me was a stranger. At least she didn't look or feel familiar to me anymore.

I made a decision that day. I was going to find the whole person I once admired and felt comfortable with. In doing so, a major overhaul was put into motion. The elimination of the daily grind that came with running my business was an important first step. That was accomplished by giving complete control of the newspaper to my assistant. Of course, in doing so, I gave up a sizeable chunk of my income. But a sufficient amount remained to allow me to live comfortably.

The agreement reached between Doug and I gave him first option to purchase the newspaper if I decided to sell after my six-month hiatus. Which at the time, I was certain selling would be the result. I wasn't so certain anymore.

The elimination of stress was only one part of my lifestyle change. I was adamant about losing the forty extra pounds I'd been lugging around since shortly after my first major lifestyle change, which was to quit smoking. A daily exercise regimen was part of the solution to the weight gain. To feel productive was something I needed for my emotional well-being. The "on foot" paper route was the answer to both. The icing on the cake was being able to replace my suits and heels with sneakers and jeans. A remarkable benefit to the comfort zone.

Mitch was the one who coerced me into changing my diet. Eliminate the fat in what you eat, and the weight will go off much faster, he had told me. A change in my diet was the biggest challenge for me. With my injury and inability to walk off the flab, I'd have to stick to Mr. Know-It-All's advice to do away with the fat, or suffer the consequences and continue shopping in the women's full-figure section of department stores.

I punched in Joe's telephone number next. It didn't surprise me that I didn't get an answer. Although I thought *she* might have picked up. A third call to set up an appointment to have my ankle X-rayed was next on my mental list of calls to be made. But since my ankle was numb by that time, I decided it was the perfect opportunity to make my way upstairs and change out of my torn jeans.

By the time that was accomplished, the numbness had faded. I could also put a little pressure on the foot without the sensation of bullets shooting up the outer side of my leg. This led me to believe I was in good enough shape to drive properly again.

TEN

JUST BECAUSE I BOTCHED my plan to get inside Joe's house and have a look around, did not have to mean the end to my snooping. That is why I drove into town to the police station.

Before I parked on one of the vacant spots outside the borough building, I made a quick survey sweep to make sure Mitch's pickup wasn't around. His truck wasn't in sight, so I parked my car.

I was hobbling to the door of the brick structure that was formerly used as a train station, when I heard a familiar voice calling my name from somewhere behind me.

"Thought that was you," Bill Miller said, and smiled over at me as he pulled the door open for me.

"Doug give you the day off, huh?"

"I'm working. Besides, Doug doesn't give us hard-working reporters a much needed day off like you did, Mrs. Cunningham."

Bill wasn't being sincere. He was being his usual suck-up-to-the-boss self.

My own words gave me a sudden shake. That was the way the old Fay Cunningham's mind worked. Always thinking people were complimentary to me because they wanted something in return. There always had to be an ulterior motive for their kindness. People didn't say what naturally came to mind anymore.

"So you're here on a story then?" I questioned.

"The new printer one of the local clubs donated. Supposed to simplify work around here for the boys."

It took a deep, deep breath, and a silent order to myself to remain calm when I really wanted to chew him out good. To demand to know what he was wasting his time on such trivial material for, when he should be hounding every officer on the force for an inside scoop on the murder case. The story about the donated printer could wait. Or I should say, would wait if I were still running the paper.

But you're not, that irritating inner voice reminded.

If nothing else, the voice did make me see I was also wasting precious time myself. There would be other days to chew the fat with Bill. I had important business to tend to.

"Can't wait to see the picture you get," I said,

making reference to the camera he was swinging at his side.

I managed to put some distance between us when I spotted Francie. Francie might only be the meter reader, but she knows everything that goes on inside the walls of this building.

"Hey, how's it going, Francie?"

"Goin' just fine on this end."

After giving my foot a glance, she parked a hand on a wide hip and gave a roll of her dark eyes.

"Looks like things ain't so fine for you," she said.

"Just a sprain. Think I can survive it."

"Lean on me," she said, pointing her elbow my way.

I did, and was being guided around and back in the direction of the door again.

"Where we going?"

Her usual deep voice softened when she finally answered. "I need a smoke."

We were outside, standing beneath the brilliant rays of noon sunshine. Francie pulled a pack of cigarettes from her shirt pocket, offered me one, and went ahead and lit one for herself, after I hesitantly and very reluctantly refused the offer. She took a long drag on the cigarette before she told me the real reason for our departure from the building. "Too many ears in there for you to be askin' me about the murder."

"How'd you know that's what I came here for?"

We exchanged looks and I had my answer. Francie knew me as well as she did the boys in uniform she worked around.

"So, what's the story?"

"Don't know. The state boys got this one. Ethel was found outside the borough limits."

Stupid. Stupid. Sometimes you should try using that mass of mush between your ears, old gal, that inner voice badgered. If I had, I would have known Ethel's case was in the hands of the state police.

But wait a minute, Mitch never told me the exact location of the refrigerator, in which Ethel's body was found. The only thing he mentioned was the woods and someone's dump site. When I remembered that, I felt a little better about myself. So just maybe I was smarter than I gave myself credit for.

"Did hear, though," Francie said with another deep inhale that I took with her. Only, I didn't taste or feel the smoke drifting down to my lungs.

And, oh, how I wanted to.

"The boys have them a lead in crackin' the case," she finally finished with her exhale.

My eyes widened. I didn't need a hit of nicotine to the system. The adrenaline was beginning to pump through me. And I was too impatient to wait for Francie to enjoy another deep drag to hear the details.

"So what is it?"

"That I don't know."

I felt like someone stuck me with a pin, bursting the bubble of anticipation. The sensation was worse than not experiencing a hit from her cigarette. When I saw Mitch's pickup turn into the parking lot, the pin hole was sealed before I could blink.

"Look, Francie, I gotta go, but if you hear any—"

"Yeah, I'll keep you posted."

I had the door to my car opened, thinking I was going to make it inside and off the lot without any kind of exchange with Mitch. I thought wrong.

ELEVEN

"I KNOW YOU SEEN ME, FAY."

His words banged into me from behind and I shot to attention. Then I slowly tilted my head so I was facing him.

"Could be I was trying to sneak off like a snake. Like you did this morning."

"You ever give it a thought I might a left like that for your benefit. Maybe I don't want a see you get hurt. Maybe even…

"We don't know what we're dealin' with, Fay. You get what I'm sayin' here?"

If I hadn't been so furious with him, I might have thanked him on the spot for being so concerned with my safety. But I was mad. And this old gal didn't need a man to protect her from the evils of the world.

"Get this, Mitchell Malone, I'll be the one to look out for Fay Cunningham. And I'd appreciate it if you'd keep that in the front of that narrow mind of yours from here on."

I hoped he understood when I slid in behind the wheel and slammed the door, it was meant to mean, *take that.*

As I backed the car around and headed for the street, I remembered something important I had forgotten to do. I not only went to the police station to see what I could find out about Ethel's murder, but fully intended to see what steps could be taken in the disappearance of my friend, Joe Wise. Even I was smart enough to know a missing person bulletin wouldn't be sent across the wire. I mean, first it would have to be proven Joe was actually missing. Which in the end, probably wasn't a job for the police. It was my job to prove he had mysteriously vanished. The police certainly weren't going to investigate my theory that something didn't feel right. And that Joe's new housekeeper was lying. She did tell the truth about Joe not being home last night. His car was gone. And I did check the house. So she hadn't lied about that. Yesterday when she said Joe was napping, and later when she said he was having his bath, she had lied. The only problem was, I couldn't prove it.

So it wouldn't have done me any good to talk to an officer about Joe anyway. At least not yet. But I would. Just as soon as I had proof. Something concrete that would give the police reason for action.

As I drove back to Joe's place, something else occurred to me. Mitch said Angel told him Joe left on a trip. So just when did he leave? If it was yesterday, I'd have proof she lied to me. *So what, we all tell a few from time to time,* that pesky inner voice pointed out. I had to agree. We all bend the truth on occasion. But why had Angel Adams? Just what was she hiding?

TWELVE

I REALLY DIDN'T EXPECT my soft taps on Joe's back porch door to be answered. But the door slid open and I was looking up into doll-eyes.

"Joe has gone out of town" I was told in the same flat, emotionless tone I was growing accustomed to.

"Well where'd he go? And when's he coming back?"

An impatient release of breath came from her before her, "I really do not know."

The door was sliding shut, but it stopped on my sneaker I shoved inside.

"I think you do," I told her, holding my breath she wouldn't put pressure on the door. On my sore foot.

"If you don't believe me, perhaps you'd like to search the house again."

"Perhaps I would. But you know what, I think I'll leave that for the police."

When her eyes narrowed, I knew I had her worried. I also had a feeling she might be more willing to answer my questions now. "You want to tell me now where Joe is? Or will it be the police?"

"I can't tell what I do not know. But if you feel it necessary to bring the police, then that's what you should do."

I did not expect her cool response, and was still too stunned to react quickly enough before the door crashed into my foot. I have no idea what kept me from screaming out in pain.

When she pulled the door in, I yanked my foot back a split second before it took another smack when the door banged shut. There were stars in front of me. Or at least, little flecks of light before the black curtain started to come down. I vaguely remember latching on to the porch railing before I sank all the way down on my knees. Try as I might, my knees touched wood before I was able to pull myself back up. I was afraid to put pressure on my foot, but I was more fearful of having my back to the pair of eyes I sensed behind me.

With the help of the railing, I hopped off the porch. That's when I knew I was in trouble. I am the first to admit I was not born blessed with coordination. To try and hop several yards across the backyard to my car would be disastrous, which left me with the option of putting my foot down and dragging it along with me.

There was the other choice. But this old gal refused to drop down on all fours and crawl to my destination. I was back to driving with my body shifted to the right on my seat so I could use my left foot on the gas and brake pedals.

My sneaker was off and I had a clear view of the swelling around my ankle. As I brought the car to a stop at the end of Popular Avenue, I took a moment to debate where I should go. The most sensible thing to do was drive straight to the hospital emergency room so I could have the ugly looking foot X-rayed. Since I suffered breaks numerous times before, I was ninety-nine percent certain the diagnose would be a sprain. Stay off the foot and ice it down several times a day for the next several, is what the doctor on duty would tell me.

After Doctor Cunningham finished her own analysis, it came time to eliminate one of the other two places I considered going. I knew I should go home and rest the foot. And I may have, if my stomach hadn't started growling for food.

The local gossip corner is where I drove to. Quieting my stomach probably carried more weight in this decision than the need to satisfy the curiosity that had been gnawing away at me.

With a little luck though, one of the state troopers

who frequent the restaurant would be taking his lunch break, and I'd use the opportunity to pick his brain about the murder investigation.

THIRTEEN

THE PARKING LOT WAS packed. No state cruisers though. And nothing that resembled Mitch's pint-sized truck. Just because that inner voice continued to urge me to drive on home and tend to my injury, doesn't mean I paid it any attention. Because I circled around the parking lot until a car backed out and I cautiously maneuvered my big Lincoln into the empty slot.

A few hops and I used the hood of a car to catch myself when I lost my balance. And that's how it went about three times before I was scooped up from behind by a pair of familiar arms. Or perhaps it was the scent of aftershave that was becoming so familiar? Whichever, I knew it was Mitch before I looked up into his weatherbeaten face and began my protest.

"Put me down. Just what do you—"

The remainder of my sentence was cut off, or more like drowned out, by the sound of laughter and clapping when we entered the restaurant.

My mouth spread in a wide smile, while my teeth were grinding together as he lugged me to the rear booth and plopped me down. Unlucky for him that he put me on the side so when he sat down, it was he who faced the crowd.

Nobody could see the hateful way I was glaring at the man they just finished applauding. And if I whispered, they wouldn't be able to hear my nasty comment to him of why the end booth had become his favorite. Which was so he could get drunk off the alcohol fumes drifting through the doorway of the adjoining bar.

"You two didn't go and do somethin' as crazy as get married, did yah?" Willie asked from where she appeared next to me. Right then and there, my anger appeared to jump from me and land in Mitch.

"Watch your mouth there, Willie. Married? Not this guy. I learn from my mistakes. And that big one was done and over with a long time ago."

"Are you quite finished?" I asked.

"I certainly hope so," Willie said.

Then it seemed only fair I got to go again. "The truth is, Willie, Mitch here thinks I need to be rescued about a zillion times a day. I can function quite well without the interference of an overblown male ego, though."

I think it was when Mitch started hissing that

Willie said, "I'll just get youn's some coffee," and she scurried off.

"A bag of ice too, please," I called after her before meeting Mitch's sharp gaze.

"You deserved every word."

"Of all the women I know, you are the—"

"I really wouldn't if I were you."

He didn't. Whatever the insult on the tip of his tongue, he swallowed it.

Then came the few moments of silence until Willie appeared with two steaming mugs of coffee in one hand and a bag of ice in the other. She handed the ice to me after my promise not to put it down Mitch's shirt or pants. But I have to say, the thought of doing it was tempting.

While I shifted around and positioned my foot on the seat and laid the bag of ice on it, Mitch ordered his usual midday salad. When it was my turn to tell her what I wanted, I did.

"Give me the same thing I ordered yesterday, but didn't get to eat."

Once Willie took off, I expected the familiar lecture. Mitch surprised me, though. But I'm not sure if he intentionally didn't start in about my steady diet of fat and calories, or if it was because he had something else he wanted to tell me.

I soon had my answer.

"In case you didn't know and wanted to attend, Thomas's funeral is tomorrow."

"No, I didn't know. And no, I wasn't planning to attend. The man tried to steal my business, for Pete's sake. I think I grew to despise him almost as much as Joe did."

"Guess it's safe for you to talk that way now, since it's official. The coroner ruled his death an accidental drowning. No worry of you becoming a suspect in that murder."

"I wasn't worried."

At least not about that, I silently said to myself and went ahead and sipped my coffee. Mitch sipped his as well before sitting his mug down and staring at me.

"What, is my face dirty?"

"I did a little checkin' on blondie."

"Yeah, what did you find out?"

"She was gettin' her mail at an apartment on North Front Street for the past few months. As of yesterday, her forwarding address is—"

"Joe's place."

"You already knew?"

"Not really. But I sort of guessed as much after finding her in her nightgown there last night."

"Was Joe home?"

"No. I haven't seen Joe since Tuesday. It's like he fell off the face of the earth."

Willie arrived with our food. I had half my cheeseburger and fries wolfed down before I noticed Mitch had barely touched his salad.

"Not very tasty, huh?"

"Just not hungry, I guess."

I had a strong feeling that wasn't it and said as much.

"Something on your mind?"

"How'd you hurt your ankle?"

I was just about ready to bite into a french fry, but didn't. I swallowed long and hard while I tried to figure out just how I should answer that one.

"Just walking along and turned it the wrong way."

"Uh, then it didn't happen when you jumped from one a Joe's windows this morning?"

"You're spying on me now, too?"

"Just happened to run into Anderson at the post office. Said by the time he got over there to see if you were okay, you had hobbled off. You want a tell me what in blue blazes you were doin' comin' out of that window, Fay?"

It took me an exceptionally long time to answer him.

"No. And to be quite honest, I just as soon we didn't discuss it again."

For some strange reason, Mitch didn't argue. And he didn't bring it up again during the next half hour or so we sat in the restaurant, finishing our food and sipping coffee.

We talked, too. Mitch filled me in on everything he found out about Ethel's murder. He had been right about the cause of death. Ethel suffocated. She suffered a long, terrifying end. She had been dead for a day or two when she was found. If the state boys had a lead as Francie had suggested, it was news to him. There was nothing left at the scene to try to trace back to the killer either. At least in way of material articles. Ethel was gagged with her own underwear. Her panty hose was used to tie her up. Fingerprints were almost pointless when one takes into consideration the number of partiers that area is known for. But there was one thing that might be the lead Francie heard about. One strand of hair was wrapped around Ethel's fingers. It was red and appeared to have come from a cheap wig.

FOURTEEN

ONCE AGAIN, I WAS ABLE to drive home properly.
Mitch offered to drive me, but the ice had worked
its magic again. My ankle was numb. Luckily, the
foot and toes had enough feeling to work the gas and
brake pedals. Mitch also offered to go round up a
pair of crutches for me. He'd drop them off within
the hour. Disappointment was written all over his
face when I told him that wouldn't be necessary; I
had several pairs at home.

I almost invited him over when he continued
searching for an excuse to stop by. Almost, is the
key word here though, because I didn't do it. The
deciding factor in my decision came because we had
spent thirty minutes or so together without criticiz-
ing each other. Why risk spoiling a good thing? So
I didn't.

When I pulled into the garage at home, my eyes
did a quick survey sweep over the clutter. Not a
single crutch in sight, even though I knew the last

set got tossed out here. It seemed logical to check the hall closet once I was inside the house. I found two pairs there. The old wooden pair went back into the closet. I carried the other pair into the kitchen with me.

Kitty was weaving between my legs as I attempted to sort junk mail and the important stuff. When her meows became too persistent to ignore, I temporarily gave up on the mail and opened her a can of food. With that out of the way, I carried crutches and mail into the living room and took a load off on the couch. I started going through the mail again, but couldn't concentrate. That inner voice was nudging at the brain walls, urging me to make the call.

Once I had my foot propped under a throw pillow on the coffee table, I punched in the memory numbers to Joe's place. Three rings before I heard her hello. She must have repeated the word three times before the moment of silence was upon us.

When the quiet was broken by her chilling, "I can hear you breathing, Fay," the hair on the back of my neck stood tall. The way my finger was quivering it took a second longer than it should have for it to land on the off button.

My good foot flew up and hit the coffee table at

the sound of the ring. The telephone jumped from my hand and hit the carpet. Before ring number three, I had phone in hand and at my ear. "Since we somehow got disconnected, I thought I'd call to answer the question you wanted to ask, Fay. Joe has not returned home yet."

Silence on my end.

Then, "Have a pleasant evening, Fay."

The click came from her end of the line. It wasn't until, "If you'd like to make a call, please hang up and try again," that I hit the Off button.

I willed myself to get up. To get mad. To drive on over there and order Angel Adams off Joe's property. But instead, I remained on the couch, frozen with fright.

During this brief time of paralysis to the trunk of my body, my mind was up and running at top speed. She called me by my first name. I never gave her permission to call me Fay, instead of the respectful address of Mrs. Cunningham. Not only didn't she respect her elders, but how dare she call me in the first place? How did she get my number? It's unlisted. She probably knows where I live, too. It wouldn't surprise me if she wasn't the one who followed me in the fog.

That thought is what got me off the couch,

checking every window and door in the house to make sure each and everyone was locked. I dug around in bedroom drawers until I found an ankle brace I had saved from a previous injury. Once I had it strapped on, I picked up dirty clothes scattered around the room and headed for the laundry room down the hall.

The telephone started ringing as I poured detergent into the washing machine. I sort of did this skip-hop-thing back to my bedroom.

"Hi, Mom," followed my out of breath hello.

I sank down on the edge of my bed, relieved it wasn't Angel again, but not totally at ease by the sound of my daughter's voice, either. She never called home just to check in and say hello.

"Hi, honey. Everything okay?"

"Everything's great, Mom. Just thought I'd call and let you know I won't be able to make it home this weekend."

It may not seem very motherly of me, but the first thought that crossed my mind upon hearing her news was, at least I won't be spending the entire weekend doing a month's worth of her dirty laundry.

"And I thought we'd get to shop for summer clothes" was my verbal response to her.

"We can do it next weekend. Okay?"

"Sure. So what's up with this weekend?"

Silence.

"I have a class now, Mom. How about I call you tomorrow."

"Okay."

"Oh, and Mom, you might want to check with Dad about paying the bill here at school. I won't get my final grades if he doesn't."

We exchanged good-byes and love you's, but I was fuming by the time I hung up.

The one and only responsibility Allen retained after our divorce, and he neglected to honor it. God only knew how I tolerated the man as long as I had.

I limped back to the laundry room and got the washer going before I dialed the number to Allen's law office. This also allotted me a few minutes to cool down before I placed the call. His secretary informed me Mr. Cunningham was in a meeting and could not be disturbed. Not even by his ex-wife. But she would give him the message that it was urgent he call me.

My ankle was throbbing by the time I hung up. I thought it a wise move to stretch back on the bed and prop pillows under it. At least until the clothes were ready to be switched to the dryer.

I closed my eyes and thoughts of why Alicia did

not answer my question about what she was doing over the weekend began forming. Overall, she was an exceptionally good kid. Good grades, good selection of friends, and best of all, drug free. Unlike so many of her classmates, she resisted the grunge look and remained with the clean and neat style.

A boy. She was seeing a nice, clean cut, and handsome young man. That was the only reasonable explanation for her giving up a weekend of running up my credit cards on a shopping spree.

FIFTEEN

THE SUDDEN WEIGHT ON my chest roused me from deep sleep. But it took several meows and a few paw taps to the nose before I opened my eyes to total darkness.

It was the darkness that got things shifting into high gear inside my head. I snapped my neck to the right so I was facing the glow of the red numbers on my digital clock.

8:53. It couldn't be. I couldn't have slept that long. But the black around me told me the clock gave the correct time. Kitty gave my face a swipe with her fluffy tail before hopping to the floor and up onto the windowsill. I thought I heard a downstairs door rattle when I started to sit up.

Kitty must have heard it too, by the way she leaped to the floor and sprang back up on the bed, crashing into my chest.

Then I heard it again. I reached for the light on the night stand. My fingers froze on the switch.

Should I or shouldn't I? My eyes had adjusted to the dark enough that I thought I could find my way to the door without turning on the light and alerting whoever was down there that someone was home. Then again, maybe that's exactly what I should do. Instead, I hurried to my feet and felt a thousand needles jab into my right ankle. I toppled over and hit the floor with a thud. Forget the light. The sound of my crash shook the whole house. If I was lucky, it also scared off whoever, or whatever, was trying to get inside.

What appeared to be a set of headlights flashed into the bedroom as I started to pull myself up the side of the bed. Then darkness again. When the lights flashed a second time, I dropped down on all fours and crawled like lightning to the window.

I arrived in time to catch a glimpse of brake lights before the vehicle disappeared around the downhill curve in the road a few yards past my driveway. Because I lived along a very lightly traveled road, I was certain whoever was behind the wheel of that vehicle also had been jiggling my doorknob. If I had only gotten to the window seconds quicker, I might have been able to make out the vehicle. I do believe it was a small-sized one.

Mitch. It had to be him. He probably rang the

bell. When I didn't answer, he tried the door, found it locked, figured I wasn't home, and left before my noisy fall.

There was one way to know for certain. Once I had myself up and sitting on the edge of the bed, I flipped on the light and picked up the telephone. From memory, I poked in Mitch's numbers.

He growled a hello after the second ring. The sound of his voice gave me such a start that it took a stern, "Who's there," before I located my voice.

"It's me, Mitch."

"Fay. You okay?"

I didn't answer immediately, because I wasn't sure I wanted to tell him someone just tried to get into my house. He'd insist on coming over, maybe stay the night. No, I wasn't ready for that.

"I'm fine. I just wanted to check on the time Thomas is getting buried tomorrow."

"Thought you weren't goin'."

I wasn't. But I had to give him some reason for calling at such a late hour. Late for him, that is.

"Well, I thought about it and decided I should probably attend."

"Why?"

Give me a break here, is what I thought. "I don't know, maybe Joe will be there" is what I finally said.

My own words turned on lights in my head. It was possible Joe would show. If for no other reason than to spit on his brother's grave.

Once Mitch told me the service was to be held at eleven, I thanked him and said a goodnight.

My fear had been chased away by the thought of possibly getting to finally see Joe again. I refused to consider the odds stacked against it actually happening.

I limped from my bedroom and went down the stairs on my butt, since I left the crutches in the living room earlier. But then, it was probably just as well I didn't have them in hand. With my lack of coordination, I'd no doubt lose my balance and wind up breaking my neck or something else.

The noise coming from my stomach led me into the kitchen, where I polished off a tuna salad sandwich and headed for the living room. I settled myself on the couch and picked up the remote to the television and turned it on. After some unsatisfactory channel surfing, I clicked the set back off. As I picked up the book I had started reading the night before, it occurred to me that my ex never returned my call. I thought it a great idea to disturb him at home.

After two rings, his recorded voice danced above

the soft background music. As instructed, I waited for the beep and left my message. "Allen, this is Fay. If you don't return my call, I promise to pay you a visit."

I hung up, smiling deviously. I was certain he was home, but just didn't want to be interrupted. He was probably in the sack with that blonde bimbo he calls his paralegal. Something probably went limp at the sound of my voice. I hope. I hope.

The smile remained with me when I flipped open my book and began reading and waited for the telephone to ring. Allen certainly didn't want a visit from me if there was a way to avoid it. If he was indeed home, he'd be calling within minutes.

An hour passed. My smile was long gone. I had been wrong. Allen couldn't have been home. My telephone never rang.

SIXTEEN

I GOT A FEW MORE HOURS of shut eye during the night. Before sleep came though, there were several long stretches of time when I sat with foot propped and ice on the ankle. I finished the book I started reading the night before during those times. The minutes in between, when the ankle was numb and almost pain free, I prowled the house with Kitty. Once or twice I thought I heard footsteps outside windows. Eventually, I talked myself into believing I imagined them.

When the sun came up, so was I, rummaging through my closet for something appropriate to wear to Thomas's funeral. I found an old favorite black pantsuit. It wasn't that I was in mourning that I decided to select something black. It was because it was customary for me to attend funerals in the ominous color.

I was in front of the floor length mirror in my bedroom, wearing panties and bra as I tried to pull flimsy and much too narrow slacks, over robust hips. It took several tugs and a few unpleasant words before I gave up, accepting the fact I still had a lot of walking and dieting to do before squeezing back into a size twelve.

Back in the closet, I found only skirts and dresses in the required larger size, and one I am too embarrassed to put a number beside. I settled on the shapely tuxedo dress in seasonless rayon crepe. There were surplice top buttons at the side with a trio of gold trimmed pearls. The ivory satin collar and French cuffs completed the formal design.

"Not bad," I said to my reflection.

Pull on a pair of dark panty hose and you'll look a whole ten pounds lighter. And that's what I did. The next problem was finding something suitable, and wide enough, to fit over my slightly swollen right foot.

Heels would give my pudgy legs length and sex appeal, but comfort is what interested me. So I slipped into black suede loafers. My collar-length dark hair was given a few added twists with the curling iron. The face was touched up with powder, mascara and lipstick. Then this old gal was all dressed up with no place to go. At least not at eight o'clock in the morning.

KITTY GOT FRESH WATER and food. Her litter was scooped with extreme caution. I didn't want to get little clumps of waste on my nice duds and have to go through the frustration of finding something else to wear all over again.

I was tempted to start making telephone calls next. First Joe, then Allen, maybe the newspaper. Or I could take a load off the foot and read the weeks' worth of newspapers stacked on the kitchen table. At the same time I could ice the ankle. But it really was feeling better. Enough so that I only limped on every third step or so.

Then I had a better idea of how to kill the next couple of hours.

SEVENTEEN

I DROVE TO THE LOCAL gossip corner and arrived
before the usual stragglers from the breakfast crowd
had cleared out. I had a seat at the rear booth that
seemed a favorite to only Mitch and me. Willie was
beside me with coffee and a compliment on my
dress by the time I got situated in my seat.

Then she told me, "You just missed your buddy."

"Mitch?"

"Um-huh. Said he was on his way to do a little
investigatin' work."

I think it was the sudden flashback of the last
time I began making demands on Willie to relin-
quish private information, and the scare I gave her,
that I was able to conceal my throbbing curiosity. I
knew it was best to ease into the question I desper-
ately wanted answered. So I sipped my coffee
before the casual inquiry.

"And did Mitch happen to mention just what he
was investigating?"

"Nah. Probably has somethin' to do with whatever he was whisperin' to the state boys about, though. So you want breakfast? Got some fresh home fries on the grill."

"Bring me some. And my usual eggs over easy and bacon too."

"Comin' right up," Willie promised with a wink and smile before heading out for the kitchen.

This day, I sat facing the customers. But there was nobody I recognized. Or more correctly, no one I wanted to strike up a conversation with. So I sat alone and had a silent conversation with myself. I asked myself what Mitch was off investigating. Then I went ahead and answered myself with more questions. Maybe a good citizen came forward who had seen Ethel with someone prior to the murder? Or maybe more evidence was collected from the crime scene that had been overlooked earlier? Or could it be that something turned up concerning the strand of cheap red wig hair found wrapped around Ethel's fingers?

After a short while, Willie returned with a plate of delicious looking food. She was about to take off again to fetch me more coffee when I asked her to hold up a minute.

"Willie, you didn't happen to hear any of the

state troopers talking about Ethel's murder, did you?"

She glanced toward her remaining customers and dropped in the seat across from me. Then she leaned close, eyes wide, as if she was going to reveal a deadly secret.

"They're thinkin' it was a woman that done it," she whispered. "They found 'em a real long piece a hair, you know."

"That's why they think it was a woman?"

"One a the reasons." She took a quick peek over her shoulder, then finished in a tone so soft I had to strain to hear. "Tests are bein' done, but they're almost sure the sleeve of Ethel's dress had lipstick on it. You knew the old girl, Fay. She never wore a lick a makeup her whole life…"

Willie scurried off to the sound of someone at the other end of the restaurant hollering for more coffee while I poked a fork into a fried potato.

What Willie said made sense. The lipstick on the sleeve gave reason to assume Ethel's killer could have been a woman. But who? Ethel had no enemies. And there certainly wasn't a woman alive that I knew, who would want to do harm to such a good-hearted and kind old soul. But there was one woman I didn't know very well. The truth is, I knew nothing about Angel Adams, other than she was Joe's new housekeeper.

As much as the glass-eyed doll gave me the creeps, I really couldn't picture her as Ethel's killer. I mean, it was not comprehendible for me to believe she would kill a woman just to take over her position as a housekeeper.

The thought was ludicrous. Of course there are people who kill over a measly few bucks. But I had strong doubts Angel was one of them. She seemed too smart to do something so stupid. No, Angel Adams would not kill Ethel for her housekeeping job. But what if there was another reason?

EIGHTEEN

I TOOK MY TIME EATING breakfast for a change. But it had very little to do with allowing myself the pleasure to taste and enjoy each bite. My thoughts were too preoccupied with Joe to enjoy anything.

By the time I left the restaurant, I had nearly an hour on my hands before it would be time to attend Thomas's funeral. It was while I sipped my third and last cup of coffee that I made up my mind how I'd spend the extra time.

I drove to the rear of Joe's property. Before stepping out of the car, my eyes took in my surroundings. The only human in sight was Mr. Anderson. He was in his flower garden with his back to me. The perfect opportunity to quietly leave the car and tiptoe over to the garage. To be more accurate, I moved on my left toes and drug the right foot along.

I didn't care who saw me return to my car after I discovered two empty parking stalls inside the garage. I even pulled the car door shut with a bang. That was done in the event Angel was peering out a window. Let her wonder what I'm doing.

For a few seconds I considered laying on the horn, but decided that might be going too far and drove off quietly. I headed into the business district of town, cruising the main streets in hopes of spotting Francie. No Francie, but there were plenty of parking tickets on windshields along Front Street.

The thought of going into the police station crossed my mind. But that's as far as it went. If Francie was inside the borough building, it might look suspicious for her to lead me outside a second day in a row. Especially since most of the guys in uniform knew who I was and how persistent I could be when I was after a story.

I pulled into the parking lot of the funeral parlor a few minutes before eleven. At first, I thought I should have driven farther north to the only other building in town that temporarily housed the dead. Besides my Lincoln, only one other car took up parking space. Then I saw the younger of Allen's two secretaries round the corner of the building and strut up the steps and go inside. At least there was one thing Allen hadn't changed after taking up with that skinny young paralegal of his. Whenever an important client passed away, someone from the office was sent on Allen's behalf to offer condolences. It looked good in case he one day decided to enter the political arena and run for district attorney or county judge. Too bad he had forgotten to stay on the good side of me. I was still alive. I also could mean a political nightmare for him when my newspaper endorsed one of his opponents, should he decide to enter politics. If there wasn't a message from him on my answering machine when I arrived home, another kind of nightmare awaited him in the very near future.

My eyes began lingering on the glove compartment. Waiting for more mourners to arrive would be a perfect time for a smoke. *If you were a smoker, it would be,* that pesky inner voice reminded. *Since you no longer are, wouldn't it be wise to throw away the pack you've kept tucked out of sight all these months?*

I felt like screaming no. What if I get stranded somewhere someday and chances for a rescue are next to none? I'd have every right to spend my last moments inhaling the deadly smoke.

The odds of that kind of tragedy ever occurring was not only rare, but a poor excuse for keeping the pack of cigarettes I had hidden. I leaned over to open the compartment to finally discard them when I saw her. Angel Adams was going up the steps of the funeral parlor's entrance. I only got a glimpse of the lean figure dressed in black, but I was certain it was her. But what in creation was she doing here?

Maybe you should go on in and ask her, Miss Pesky returned to encourage. "Just maybe I will," I said as I reached for the door handle.

NINETEEN

I ENTERED THE BUILDING and took a step back after being hit with the powerful scent of flowers. Once I got my footing again, I went ahead and signed the visitor book. In doing so, I noticed the single name Angel printed in all capitalized letters a few lines above. *How odd,* is the only thought that came to mind.

The sound of the preacher's voice coming from the podium where he stood in front of the coffin saved me from stepping up to view Thomas one last time. Or perhaps, from spitting on him like I know Joe might do if he were here. But I saw Joe wasn't here after I sank into one of the numerous vacant folding chairs in the last row of several.

Angel sat alone in the front row. Allen's secretary was seated a few rows back between two elderly men. A few other seniors and several young women sat scattered around the room.

The preacher was short on sermon and closing

prayer. Lost in private thoughts, mostly trying to figure out why Angel was here, people began to depart before I was fully aware the service was officially over. I looked around just in time to see Angel hurrying out the door. I jumped up, bringing the chair up with me. There wasn't time to be embarrassed by my situation. I needed to free my dress so I could catch up to Angel before it was too late.

Two tugs and I was free to go. Only, a large section of my dress remained behind. I ignored the stares and whispers as I did my skip-hop-thing to the door.

By the time I got outside, Angel was gone. A few cuss words were said under my breath as I limped to my car. I not only had missed my chance to confront Angel, but had ruined the dress I planned to wear again when I attended Ethel's funeral.

By the time I was situated behind the wheel of my car, I thought about driving to the cemetery. There was a good possibility Angel would be there to witness Thomas lowered into the ground. But why? And why would she tell me if I confronted her?

I didn't join the small parade of vehicles to the hillside cemetery. I'm not sure why, but I suddenly felt the need to see Mitch.

Perhaps he could shed some light on why doll-eyes had attended Thomas's funeral. Or it just could be that I wanted to share this information with him in hopes he would share any new information he had on the investigation into Ethel's murder.

I drove around town to some of Mitch's regular haunts, but didn't see his truck anywhere. So I headed for his small farm outside of town. His truck wasn't parked outside the sun-bleached, two-story wood house or behind the makeshift barn. But I gave the front door a try anyway. It was locked and no one answered the several raps I gave the door.

I headed back toward town, thinking I'd take another spin through. If not Mitch, maybe I'd spot Francie. Never in my wildest imagination did I expect to pass Joe's old Mercedes on Broadway.

TWENTY

THANKFULLY, NOBODY was tailing me or I would have been rear-ended when I slammed on the brakes. By the time I got turned around and pulled onto the rear of Joe's property, enough time had passed for me to consider I had imagined seeing him. But as I started out of my car, I saw Joe coming out of the garage, an overnight bag in hand and brushing against the leg of his trousers.

"Joe… It really is you," I said, a relieved smile widening my mouth.

"Of course it's me."

I wanted to throw my arms around him and give him the biggest bear hug he'd ever experienced. But I sensed something wasn't right with my dear old friend. And my relief at finally seeing him again was suddenly replaced with concern.

"I've been worried, Joe. Where have you been?"

"Where've you been," he tossed right back. "You're dressed like you're going to a funeral."

Before I could answer, or more like, before I was sure how to answer, Joe started up the backyard to the house.

For a few seconds, I remained where he left me; too stunned to move as a result of the cold in his voice, in his entire demeanor. What happened to the jolly old fellow who could make me smile no matter how terrible a day I was having? Who was this stranger?

He was jiggling the key in the back porch door lock, cussing up a storm by the time I joined him on the porch and offered to be of assistance. He took a few steps back and I slipped into the narrow space in front of him. One twist with the key and the knob turned. I pushed the door open and stepped aside so Joe could enter first.

"I was already to a funeral, Joe," I mentioned.

Weary eyes looked over into mine. "It was your brother, Thomas's."

"The old geezer's dead?"

My breath was stuck in my throat, which explained why I nodded him a yes instead of saying the word. I suppose I was holding my breath also so I wouldn't blurt out the terrible news about Ethel before he had a moment to fully absorb the news about Thomas.

I watched him shove aside dirty dishes on the table and plop his overnight bag down in their place before pulling out a chair and dropping himself into it.

Not only were their dirty dishes on the table, but they took up counter and sink space as well. The condition of the kitchen kept the news of Ethel at bay, while I wondered where Joe's new housekeeper was. And just what kind of a housekeeper was she anyway?

"Somebody shoot him or put a knife in him?"

Joe's question took me by surprise at first. But giving it some thought, I could understand why he assumed Thomas was murdered. The man had dealt with some really shady characters over the years; had made more enemies over those years than friends as well. This also made me remember Mitch's theory that Thomas might have had help sliding under the bath water. Mitch must have known the man a lot better than he ever led me to believe.

I pulled the chair out across from Joe and eased into it. "Nobody murdered Thomas. According to the coroner, he drowned in the bathtub, accidentally."

"Then the old geezer was lucky clear to the end."

It pained me to sit watching this stranger lost in

private thought. So I jumped up, or started to, until the jabbing sensation in my ankle reminded me of my injury. On my second attempt to stand, I was more careful. I began gathering up dirty dishes and carried them to the sink. I was expecting Joe to tell me to leave them—his new housekeeper would take care of the mess. But Joe remained silent, which seemed to give me the go ahead to bring up the subject of his new housekeeper.

"Some new housekeeper you've hired, Joe. I've never seen this place so—"

"What new housekeeper?"

TWENTY-ONE

MY CENTRAL nervous system seemed to temporarily lock up like car brakes are known to do on occasion. The sound of the back door opening is what unlocked me.

I saw Angel. Joe saw Angel, and his eyes and face lit up like they used to do when he saw me.

"There's my girl," declared Joe, as he jumped up with the energy of a young man, and threw his arms around skin and bones.

All I could do was stand and watch this display of affection. I think my temporary paralysis was partially due to the doll-eyes glaring at me. The other part was because I was totally baffled.

My confusion was soon put on hold when Joe pulled back from her, and looked over at me.

"Fay, have you met Angel?"

I cleared my throat aloud, about to get the letters to a yes to topple off my lips, when Angel answered for me.

"Yes, we've met."

Joe was gently pulled around so his back was to me. I'm sure this maneuver was done so he wouldn't see the threatening look Angel was giving me.

"Listen, why don't you go on upstairs and get changed," Angel said. "Then you can tell me all about your trip."

I can't believe I actually stood there and said nothing while I watched Angel guide Joe out of the kitchen and head him in the direction of the stairs. But I did. I even remained rooted to my position in front of the sink when Angel returned and suggested I stop back at a later time—after Joe had time to rest up from his trip.

Fay Cunningham listened to every word uttered without one interruption. But when Angel finished with me, words were waiting to shoot from my mouth. "Just what is going on around here? And please don't test my intelligence by playing dumb."

"I don't play, Fay" I was told in one level breath. "Now I really must insist you leave."

The door was held for my exit. One I didn't want to make, but felt it best I did. Especially after what I had witnessed between her and Joe.

"Okay. You win this time. But I want you to remember, I will be back."

The door swished shut, nearly smacking me in the fanny as I crossed the threshold. I looked over my shoulder several times on my way to the car. I didn't see them, but I could feel her eyes on me. It was all I could do to resist the urge to wave my middle finger back at her before I ducked inside my car.

STEAM BEST DESCRIBES what I was feeling when I pulled away from Joe's property. I did lay on the horn this time when I drove off. At the stop sign, I banged my hands against the steering wheel a little too hard and gave out an ouch.

I think it was as I began rubbing my palms together to take away the stinging sensation that some of my anger began subsiding. As the anger left, the brain kicked a few things around. I never did get to tell Joe about Ethel. The other woman who put a glow in Joe when she walked within eye range. It may sound cruel, but telling Joe his long-time housekeeper and companion had been murdered could just be the answer to breaking whatever spell Angel Adams had put him under.

Rest time's up, Joe. Fay Cunningham's about to pay you another visit.

TWENTY-TWO

I FELT PUMPED UP and pain free as I marched up Joe's backyard to the porch door. Forget ladylike knuckle taps on the door. I used both fists and pounded, determined not to be ignored or turned away.

"All right," Angel hissed as she yanked open the door.

"I'm back as promised," declared I, and shoved her aside and entered the kitchen.

Joe entered the room at the same time.

"What's all the commotion down here?" he demanded.

I saw Angel open her mouth to speak, but beat her to it.

"I don't know why, but Angel here's been passing herself off as your housekeeper, Joe."

Angel immediately responded to the way Joe's eyes seemed to question her.

"I didn't know if you were ready to tell people yet."

"For heaven's sake, child, I want to shout from rooftops that I have a daughter."

"Daughter?"

"Yes," said Joe. "Angel is my daughter. Not my housekeeper, Fay."

The news floored me. I suppose it was because I was in a state of shock that I allowed Angel to guide me to a table chair.

"I'm sorry, Fay. I really hated not telling you the truth. But Father left so suddenly that it wasn't clear to me how he planned to handle the news of having a daughter."

By the time she finished her sweet little confession, the three of us were seated around the table.

"I did leave rather abruptly," Joe admitted. "And I accept full responsibility for the misunderstanding."

It may have been my turn to speak, but I was not yet ready to do so. The truth is, I was not yet able to work tongue and mouth well enough to form words.

Then Joe took my turn. "I am surprised at you, Fay. How could you believe I hired a new housekeeper? You of all people should know I wouldn't think of replacing Ethel."

You better start, I wanted to say, but didn't. And it wasn't because I was still too much in shock to speak. I just didn't want to break the terrible news that way.

"Actually," Angel began, "Fay did not believe I had been hired to replace Ethel."

"Am I correct, Fay?"

This time I listened to that inner voice.

"You are correct. But when I learned Ethel had been—"

I cut myself off. I just didn't have the heart to break Joe's with the single word, murder. There had to be an easier way. Even though Joe was going to be devastated no matter what word I used.

"Ethel had been what?" Joe asked, his features showing signs of alarm.

I looked over at Angel, thinking maybe she'd want to break the news. But then, the anxious look on her face convinced me she didn't know Ethel had been murdered either.

After swallowing long and hard, I attempted to answer Joe's question.

"Ethel is gone, Joe."

"Gone. Gone where?"

"She's passed on," I answered softly, and reached across the tabletop for his hand.

He latched on to my hand so tightly that it was all I could do to keep from screaming at him to let go. I saw tears come into his eyes and experienced my own vision clouding over.

I was too busy concentrating on Joe to notice Angel's immediate reaction to my news. But her, "Oh, I'm so sorry, Father," that came within seconds, sounded sincere. Then she was out of her seat caressing the man's shoulders before her next breath.

I suppose I should feel grateful that Joe let go of my hand so he could reach up and pat one of hers. But I did not feel grateful. I felt betrayed. Okay, jealous. One love tap from Angel and Joe forgot I was sharing air space with them.

Before that pesky inner voice had a chance to insist it would be bad timing and mean spirited to interrupt the touchy scene between father and daughter, I went ahead and did it.

"Ethel was murdered, Joe."

That got his attention. And just maybe prevented him from sinking into a state of depression. I say this because his hand returned to the table with a bang. He sat tall, eyes blinking back tears before he looked straight over into mine.

"What do you mean, Ethel was murdered?" he demanded.

I told him about how she had been tied up, gagged, and stuffed inside an old refrigerator in the woods. I gave him the coroner's ruling that she died of suffocation. I did not tell him this probably took a while to occur. Or that it had to have been a slow and terrifying death for her. But then, Joe is no dummy.

During all this, Joe would occasionally shake his head no in disbelief and Angel would massage his shoulders a little harder. Her expression was saying, *how awful,* the entire time I spoke.

When I finished, she said the words.

"It just can't be so," Joe finally said. "Why would anyone want to hurt my Ethel?"

I vividly remember the way Angel's expression hardened when Joe made reference to Ethel as *my* Ethel. My first thought at seeing this was, *the glass-eyed doll is jealous.*

TWENTY-THREE

ONCE I TOLD JOE I HAD heard the services were to be held for Ethel in the morning, but I wasn't sure of time or location, I agreed with Angel's suggestion he go lie down for a while. Angel went ahead and helped him up the stairs to his bedroom while I let myself out of the house.

By the time I was back in my car and driving, the afternoon was pretty well shot. I still had places to go, people to see, but I headed for home. I needed time to rest, to think, to churn things around inside my head. I also needed to get out of the dress and panty hose. And for the first time in hours, my ankle was throbbing.

MAIL GOT TOSSED on the counter. Kitty got fed and watered. Then I headed upstairs to change into jeans and sneakers. Before the change though, I switched day old wet clothes from washer to dryer. I used the banister for support as I went down the steps and limped back into the kitchen. It took a few moments to decide if I should go for ice packs in the freezer or look next door in the refrigerator for food.

It was during those brief moments that I stood at the counter debating my decision that I noticed the red light blinking on the answering machine. I hit the message button and opened the refrigerator door to start digging around for something quick and easy to prepare. The search ended with the sound of Alicia's voice.

"Mom, I can't come home this weekend because… I'm getting married, Mom."

"No you are not," I responded fiercely before it dawned on me I had shouted to a recording. "That will be solved real quick," I said to Kitty, who was busy sniffing her food. Then I picked up the phone and punched in the numbers from memory to my daughter's dormitory room.

I waited and waited for someone to answer one of the dozen or so rings. No one picked up. And it was obvious Alicia had turned off her answering machine intentionally. Smart girl. She knew I'd be calling, of course.

BY THE TIME I got my Lincoln backed out of the driveway, the sun was nowhere to be seen. Those monstrous clouds from Wednesday appeared to have rolled back into town to dump another round of misery.

TWENTY-FOUR

ALLEN'S OFFICE is located in the business district of town. Since it was Friday afternoon, I should have known every parking space along the one way southbound street would be taken. I spotted a woman getting into her car a few spaces down from Allen's office building. I made a quick left at the light and circled back around the block. Just as I turned off Broadway and back onto Front Street, the woman whipped her little Toyota into the late afternoon traffic.

With fingers crossed on the steering wheel, I asked for some heavenly intervention. "Please. Please keep the space open till I get there."

The car ahead of me slowed to a crawl as it approached the vacant parking space. I was just about to curse it when the driver seemed to change his mind and speed on by.

I thought it only appropriate to glance heavenward and issue a sincere "thank you" before putting complete concentration on what I was doing, which was trying to back a very large car into a very short space to the tune of horns honking to my left and rear. With the mission accomplished, I gave out a heavy sigh of relief.

Then I was ready to make a mad dash for the brick three story sandwiched between two others. But before I slid over onto the passenger's seat to get out on that side, I reminded myself I had an ankle injury. Just because a torrential downpour began smacking into everything in its path, didn't mean I should risk further injury by trying to keep from getting drenched. I did pay close attention to where I was stepping, but I didn't waste any time getting myself under the roof, either.

THE PRETTY YOUNG THING at the reception desk started to look up at me with a smile, until she got a good look at me. I'm not sure her face soured by the way I must have looked, or if it was because she recognized me as Allen's ex. I didn't really care much what thought went through her little blonde head. I had important business to take care of.

"Is Allen here?"

"Sorry. He's away at a meeting," I was told.

"He will be returning to the office today though, right?"

"Hello, Fay," Miss Husband Stealer greeted as she strolled up beside me.

"I need to see Allen" is how I greeted her. Then demanded, "Do you know where he is?"

"He is in a meeting. But he should be back—" She cut herself off long enough to look at her diamond studded gold wristwatch. *Probably a gift from my love-struck ex.* "Half hour, tops. If you'd like, I can have him call—"

"I'll wait."

"Suit yourself," she said before polished and perfectly straight teeth flashed when she smiled.

I watched her wiggle down the hallway and weave into an office. Then I looked around to the cushioned chairs behind me. I was tempted to fall into one, give the foot a rest, dry off, but I couldn't do it. Too many mixed emotions were storming through me to spend the next half hour being observed from near and far by Allen's enticing blonde workers.

I made my way back to the car. As I pulled the door shut behind me on the passenger's side, I eyed the glove compartment. My tongue slowly moistened upper, then lower lip, as I stared. That was before I looked around like a kid sneaking candy before a meal. Seeing the coast was clear, I opened

the compartment and latched onto the pack of cigarettes. Another quick peek to my left and right as
I slid back over behind the wheel.

My fingers had the pack of smokes ripped open
before the conclusion of the flash of lightning
outside the car. I could taste-smell the lit cigarette
before I had it situated between my fingers. For a
split second, I gave thought to what I was doing. The
next second, my lips closed around the filter tip,
while my index finger pushed in the car's cigarette
lighter.

If my lips hadn't dried fast to the cigarette, I know
it would have fallen from my mouth with the unexpected tapping sound on the passenger's side window.

The instant I saw Mitch, the thought of hitting the
main button that locked the doors torpedoed through
my head. But the way water was running off the tip
of his cowboy hat, I took pity on him and kept my
finger off the button.

Mitch took his hat off and tossed it on the floor
before he dove inside. As he straightened up in the
seat, the cigarette lighter popped back, signaling it
was ready to burn.

I didn't reach for it, but Mitch did. He raised it
to the tip of the cigarette still hanging from my
mouth, but didn't touch red circle glow to tobacco

and paper. He did offer words of encouragement. "Go ahead. It's the answer to all your problems."

Our eyes temporarily locked in conversation.

I am the one who blinked first and proceeded to slowly remove the cigarette from between my lips. Then I looked over into midnight-blue eyes. Our mouths exchanged these little smiles.

"How is it you always seem to show up just at the right moment, Mitchell Malone?"

His answer came by way of the arm he slid around my shoulder and used to draw me close. We stayed like that, me with my head on his chest, him with his arm around me, holding me close, saying nothing, while rain slashed and crashed around us.

"Feeling better?" Mitch said several minutes later.

I tilted my head back so I was looking up into a contented face. "My daughter's eloping this weekend."

TWENTY-FIVE

BY THE TIME MITCH digested my news and started to comment, I cut him off when I jerked up in my seat. I was certain I saw Allen under the big black umbrella that bobbed past the car window. There was only one way to be sure though.

"I'll be right back," I told Mitch as I crawled over him to the tune of a few oohs and aahs when my knee squeezed down on one of his inner thighs.

WATER DRIPPED FROM my hair, nose and clothes when I limped up to Allen's receptionist, who appeared to be tidying up her desk before calling it a day.

When she looked up at me, I almost expected her to offer the name and number of her hairdresser. But I didn't give her the chance. "He is here now, right?"

She nodded a yes, but forgot the polite smile that was supposed to go with the job. I headed for the closed door at the end of the narrow hallway. Or I should say, I steam dried myself as I motored toward that closed door. I didn't bother knocking once I arrived either. Proper manners were the last thing on my mind when I pushed open the door.

Allen was behind his polished oak desk, looking as if he was enjoying a telephone conversation, until he looked up and made eye contact with me.

Before he could finish his "I'll have to call you back," my finger pushed in the telephone button and disconnected the call.

"I don't recall today's weather report including hurricane Fay in its forecast."

"Don't be cute with me, Allen."

"Clever maybe. But cute, I don't think so," he said with an arched, and professionally shaped dark eyebrow.

"Have you heard from Alicia?"

"I sent a check to the school this morning, Fay."

"You could have called and told me."

He sat taller, straightened his flashy tie, then looked up at me in a way I recognized immediately. I had seen that guilt-ridden look before.

"Maybe I wanted to see you. To tell you—"

For a moment there, I wanted to slide my arms around those familiar broad shoulders and tell him I understood. That I accepted his apology for walking away from the fairy tale life we had been leading. But when he told me it was over between him and Dana, and that he realized now he made a horrendous mistake with us, I went cold.

I think what happened was, I had a flashback of all the suffering his affair and the divorce had brought me. Some compassion had survived though, because I did say I was sorry for the breakup between him and young blondie, and that it was a shame it couldn't have happened before our divorce was finalized. Then I proceeded to pile on more bad news.

"Our daughter has gone off somewhere to get married."

"That's not funny, Fay."

"Do you see me laughing?"

Allen did the same thing I had done once he knew I wasn't joking around. He picked up the telephone and dialed her room number at school.

He got the same no answer that I had as well.

Then we spent the next hour or so huddled around his telephone calling Alicia's friends. We were looking for a clue to where our daughter might be. And just who it was she was about to commit the rest of her life to.

Regrettably, neither question got answered. It was

news to everyone we spoke to that Alicia was seeing someone on a regular basis, let alone getting married.

We finally agreed there was no one left to call. Nothing left to do at the moment. We did discuss driving out to the college, but decided it would probably be a waste of time. It was highly unlikely the newlyweds would honeymoon in Alicia's dorm. All we could do was continue calling and hope she eventually picked up her phone. Or called home.

ALLEN OFFERED TO SHARE his umbrella and walked me to my car. We said good-bye at the door with promises to keep each other posted over the weekend on any new developments.

When Allen started to reach for the door for me, I remembered Mitch and grabbed the handle first.

TWENTY-SIX

"MUST A BEEN ONE DANDY of a discussion 'tween the two of you," Mitch commented the second I slid in behind the wheel. "Was gettin' too worried to even catch me a nap."

"He wants a reconciliation," I told him as I looked straight ahead into the stormy weather.

Mitch reached down for his hat and fidgeted with it as he too stared at the rain belting against the windshield.

I was the one who finally broke the silence. "I told him no."

More silence.

"What about your daughter? You ever get around to discussin' her elopement?"

"We called everyone we could think of, but nobody knows anything. Or if they do, they aren't saying."

"Anything I can do?"

I looked over at the same time he was glancing

my way. For a second there, when our eyes met, a warm feeling washed through me. I smiled, then I answered his question with an offer. "You can come home with me. I think there's a couple of steaks in the freezer we could fix. Then maybe—"

I stopped because his eyes were already telling me no before he actually said the word.

"Have some things to take care of. Rain check, okay?"

I wanted to tell him we could do it later, after he took care of whatever business he had. But somehow I knew this evening wouldn't suit. Mitch was giving me time alone to think long and hard about my ex's proposal of reconciliation.

"Another night will be just fine," I told him. Then I watched him leave the car, huddled forward as he braved the storm.

I turned the key and flipped on the wipers so I could watch him make his way across Front Street and disappear down the alley to the municipal parking lot where his truck was parked.

I had no desire to head home to an empty house so I could think about Allen. It was Alicia and what she was on the verge of doing that consumed my thoughts as I drove east on Broadway. There was one other person who just might know something,

I decided. Joe was like a third grandfather to Alicia. She confided in him when her father or I wouldn't do. Or more specifically, when she needed an ear to bend without the threat of being talked out of something she really wanted to do.

I parked at the rear of Joe's property. Downstairs lights were on inside the house. If I was lucky, I could time it right to dash for the house during one of the brief periods when the rain eased to nearly a drizzle before it soaked everything in its path seconds later. After all, I was nearly dry from my last mad dash into Allen's office building. And it didn't make a whole lot of sense to waste time digging around in the trunk for the umbrella I kept in there with my newspaper shoulder bag and God only knew what else.

With my hand firmly gripped on the door handle, I waited for the right moment. It was near at hand. One, two, three, go. I jumped out of the car, felt my ankle start to turn, but got it straightened out before damage was done. Then I started up the backyard, a little too slow to make it to the porch before the next pounding rain struck.

Whoever was inside must have heard my feet land on the porch floor, because the door was opening as I reached up to knock. Angel greeted me with a pleasant smile and invited me inside like she would a good friend.

"Is Joe here?" I asked as I brushed dripping bangs off my forehead.

"He's visiting with Ethel's family," I was informed before Angel lit one of those long matches off the side of its box and held it to the front burner on Joe's old gas stove.

She sat the tea kettle over on the heat, and turned back to face me. "He mentioned she has a sister still living."

I nodded to acknowledge that I already knew this, then took a load off at the table after Angel told me to have a seat. "The water will be hot in a minute for tea."

"You do drink tea, don't you, Fay?"

"Yes," I said, when I was thinking that a shot of something stronger would be preferred.

"You really shouldn't bother. I have to be going—"

"Nonsense. Joe will be home soon. So you might as well wait. Besides, it'll give us some time to start fresh."

I had no desire to sip tea and shoot the breeze with this peculiar young woman. But then again, it would be the perfect opportunity to bring up a few things that had been on my mind.

For some reason, I felt it necessary to closely

watch Angel spoon loose tea into the kettle. It might sound crazy or just really paranoid, but I think I half-suspected she might slip something other than tea in there.

She didn't. At least as far as I could see. When she offered sugar, I said no thank you when I normally take two heaping spoonfuls. When she gracefully lowered her petite self onto the chair across from me, I fired off question number one.

"So tell me, Angel, how is it Joe never once mentioned having a daughter, and out of the blue, you appear?"

The question or the tone in which it was asked didn't appear to create any change in her. She sipped her tea and looked over at me without a trace of emotional upheaval showing in her expression.

"Joe had no idea he had fathered a child. I had no idea who my father was until my mother died recently."

"So did she leave you this long letter explaining things?"

"Not exactly. She kept a diary in a safe deposit box. It was all written down in there. The safety deposit box also contained my original birth certificate that names Joe as my father."

I have no idea of the amount of time that passed

while we shared tea and conversation. By my third cup of the bitter tasting brew, I was telling Angel to add my usual spoonfuls of sugar. And by the time I finally did leave Joe's house, I not only had begun to trust Angel Adams, but was also beginning to like her.

It was only after Joe returned and confessed to being totally exhausted and ready for bed that I left. But not before I watched Angel drop pills into his mouth she said the doctor prescribed to help him sleep.

TWENTY-SEVEN

THE HEAVY RAIN HAD leveled off to a drizzle by the time I drove toward home in the dark. I thought about stopping off at the local gossip corner for a bite to eat, but I had more important things to do, like track down my daughter before she made the foolish mistake of marrying a man she barely knew. Or better yet, one I hadn't been given the opportunity to approve or disapprove of.

I thought I saw Mitch's pickup pull away from my driveway as I approached. If it was him though, he was around the curve in the road before I had a close enough look to tell for sure.

If it was him, he'd be back. But I went ahead and called his farm anyway once I got inside the house and had checked the answering machine for messages. There were none.

I got Mitch's answering machine and hung up before it finished with its announcement to leave a message after the beep. Kitty was fed and given some attention before I headed up the stairs to get out of damp clothes and hit the shower.

As I stripped down to bare skin, my mind searched for answers to my daughter's whereabouts. Joe insisted he knew nothing of her seeing a boy on a regular basis. As a matter of fact, he hadn't heard from her since the last time she was home, which was almost a month ago.

When I thought about the kind of sheltered and affluent life Alicia had growing up, and how, as a result, she was probably too naive about the opposite sex, it brought Angel into my thoughts. The sad tale she told me over tea was about a childhood totally opposite Alicia's.

Angel was raised below the poverty level. Her mother had introduced a stepfather into her life when she was age two. She had very little to say about the man, but I sensed she didn't like him much. Just because the stepfather used his disability check to buy booze and gamble, and her mother worked two jobs and was never home, didn't mean they weren't a happy little family, Angel had stated. It's the tone of voice she used when she said it, and the way her features reverted back to that stone cold state I witnessed on previous occasions, that told me all was not as she wanted me to believe.

I was bending over to reach in and turn on the shower when the doorbell dinged. I grabbed the terry cloth robe from the back of the bathroom door and made it downstairs on the third ding-dong.

"Saw the lights on and figured you were here," Mitch was saying as he took off his hat and stepped inside.

"I was just about ready to hop in the shower."

"Well, go ahead. I'll wait. Put on some coffee too, if you don't mind."

"I don't mind," I said to the back of him as he started down the hall to the kitchen.

Instead of hurrying upstairs to shower and dress, I followed him to the kitchen. Something didn't feel right about him showing up on my doorstep when just a few hours ago he thought it best he stay away for the night.

"Has something happened?" I asked from the doorway, where I stood watching him fill my Mr. Coffee pot with water.

"Get your shower and we'll talk."

The way I was looking at him must have been why he said more.

"It's nothin' to get worked up about. So go on now. The coffee'll be done soon."

TWENTY-EIGHT

A FEW QUICK SWIPES with a soapy sponge in certain cracks and crevices, an extremely warm rinse, and Fay Cunningham's shower was finished.

I was in too big a hurry to bother styling the hair or cover facial age marks with makeup. I pulled on a comfortable old cotton nightshirt and robe and headed back down to the kitchen.

MITCH WAS LEFT to entertain himself for a total of fifteen minutes. I'm not sure how entertaining those minutes were for him, but by the way the table looked, he hadn't daydreamed them away either.

"Haven't you been the busy little beaver" was my way of a compliment as I sat down at the table in front of a double-decker sandwich and steaming mug of coffee.

"You might want a think about replacin' things in the frig," Mitch suggested as he sat down in the chair across from me. "You got some really scary lookin' stuff growin' in there."

I bit into tomato, lettuce and cheese, neatly layered between four slices of whole wheat bread.

"How is it?" Mitch asked as he watched me chew, then swallow, my first big bite.

"Not bad, but it'd be a lot tastier with a few slices of bacon."

He commented by way of shaking his head in disapproval before biting into his own sandwich.

I sipped my coffee, while I waited for him to finish thoroughly chewing his food before swallowing. The wait was a strain on the nerves. I survived it though in silence. But the second he swallowed, I fired away with my question. "Are you gonna tell me or not?"

When he put his mug of coffee to his lips instead of answering me right away, I wanted to kick him one under the table. But something, or more specifically, that inner voice told me that wouldn't be a smart move.

"Something's turned up on this Angel Adams," he finally mentioned.

And here I was, all puffed up, expecting big news. What a let-down.

"I already know about her being Joe's daughter," I said, and picked up my sandwich to take my disappointment out on it.

"She's Joe's daughter?"

My teeth were a hair from chomping into my sandwich when his question came. The sandwich was dropped back down on paper plate.

"That's not what you were going to tell me?"

"Angel Adams isn't Angel Adams. Her legal name is Angel Traditor. Adams was her mother's maiden name."

Mitch did take another bite of his sandwich, while I kicked a few things around in my head.

"Traditor must have been the stepdad's name. That has to be it. Angel doesn't like him, or the name, and decided to take her mom's maiden one. No crime in that."

Mitch chewed and swallowed this second bite a lot faster and had a response to my moment of thinking out loud.

"Don't know about a step dad, but there was a crime."

He took another bite of food, while I puffed up again with anticipation.

This time, I didn't have the patience to wait until he finished emptying his mouth.

"What crime?"

"Don't know. Happened when she was a juvenile. Records are sealed."

"But you're saying Angel committed a crime?"

"Yep. That's how I found out her name isn't Adams. Had the boys put her fingerprint through that there fancy new computer system of theirs."

"How did you get Angel's fingerprint?"

Mitch was back to sipping his coffee. There was also this sly grin lighting up his face and eyes.

"When I stopped by yesterday mornin' to break the news about Ethel to Joe, I got me a strange feelin' about the young woman who answered the door."

"My first impression of her wasn't a good one, either. But tonight I saw a side of her I really admired. Sounds like she had a tough childhood, Mitch."

"Yeah, and one that got her a criminal record in Portsmouth, Ohio."

"So just how did you get the fingerprint?" I asked while my mind was already trying to cough up the reason Portsmouth, Ohio sounded so familiar.

"It was quite by accident. I was pullin' my car keys out of my pocket to leave, when the little note pad I just bought dropped out. Angel picked it up for me."

"See. She can be very nice."

"Maybe. But I'd feel a lot better if I knew how she broke the law."

"Betsy."

"Betsy what?"

"She was one of the best crime reporters the paper's ever had. Last year she got married and followed her new husband to Ohio. Portsmouth, Ohio."

"I think it'd be a really good idea to give Betsy a call. But just in case Betsy doesn't come through, the state boys might."

"If the records are sealed—"

"No, not that. They sent Ethel's clothes away to be analyzed. Angel's fingerprint is on its way there now."

"You can't lift fingerprints from clothes, can you?"

"You'd be surprised what all this new technology is capable of doing."

"So you really think Angel might have had something to do with Ethel's murder?"

"I'm not rulin' her out."

"But why would she do it?"

"Didn't have that figured out till you said she was Joe's daughter." I'm sure Mitch saw in my expression his answer hadn't satisfied me. Or better still, had only piled on more confusion.

"She kills Ethel because she wants Joe all to herself."

Too bad Mitch hadn't witnessed the two of them together. Angel took a backseat to no one in Joe's eyes, Fay Cunningham included.

TWENTY-NINE

WE FINISHED OUR SANDWICHES and the pot of coffee before Mitch said goodnight. Polishing off all that coffee took some time, and a lot more communicating. A little bit of everything was discussed. In the end, questions went unanswered. Situations unresolved. Yet I hated to see Mitch go.

Maybe he didn't have the answer to why Alicia made the decision to elope. And so what if he couldn't be convinced Angel was not capable of cold-blooded murder. He was good company on a stormy spring night.

After countless cups of tea and then coffee, my system had enough caffeine floating around in it that it would take a week before I was ready for anything that resembled a sound sleep. So I gathered the newspapers that had piled up on a corner of the table and carried them into the living room. I dropped the newspapers on the middle couch cushion before settling on the end one. Right foot got propped on pillows on the coffee table before I was fully situated.

As I opened the most recent paper, Kitty decided it was time to curl up on my lap. This, of course, made it difficult to spread out the paper. So I didn't. I gave Kitty a gentle neck massage with one hand, while the other one worked the remote to the television set. After flipping through the channels, I settled on an old movie I'd seen before and liked, but for the life of me couldn't remember the title.

Kitty's tiny motor was cranked on high. But as she purred with contentment, restlessness grew within me. It was going on eleven. A late hour to begin making telephone calls.

I called Alicia's dorm first. Like earlier, no one picked up the dozen or so rings before I clicked off.

The thought of calling Allen wouldn't go away even after I told myself I wasn't going to call him. If he'd heard from Alicia, he would have called. That was what we agreed on. And we had nothing else to discuss.

But there was still this longing to call.

Fight it, I ordered myself. He cheated on you once. He'll do it again. It's over. The divorce papers say it's over. You can't go back. You must go forward.

"I'm trying, darn it."

The sound of my voice sent Kitty to the floor. My, "I'm sorry honey, come on back up," got me nowhere. I soon knew the apology and coaxing was just unacceptable. Kitty sulked off and out of the room without so much as a look back at me.

The thought did cross my mind that it wasn't the sound of my voice that peeved her, so much as it was what I was thinking. Because I do have these moments when I am convinced she understands what I'm thinking and feeling. So it just could be that she wanted to distract my thoughts away from Allen. Maybe she knew it wouldn't be long before I'd have myself seriously considering a reconciliation with him.

Her pouting stunt worked, because when I did start tapping out numbers on the telephone, they weren't Allen's.

THIRTY

BETSY WAS A NIGHT OWL like me. So I didn't antici-
pate a problem calling at such a late hour.

Her hello came after the second ring. "Betsy, it's
Fay."

"Fay? Oh, Fay, what's wrong?"

"Nothing. How are you, kiddo?"

"I'm pregnant. Isn't that great news?"

"How pregnant?"

"Something is wrong."

"No. I just wanted you to do me a small favor.
But in your condition—"

"I'm not disabled, Fay. I'm having a baby. So
what do you need?"

For a brief second, I considered forgetting the
whole thing. It wasn't right to impose on Betsy, on
her new life, in a new town, with a new husband,
and now a baby on the way. But in the next second,
I remembered the very big favor I had done for her.
Not only had I written a glowing recommendation

letter for her, but I had called the publisher of the newspaper out there in Ohio where she wanted to go to work. I told him what a tremendous asset Betsy would be to his paper. I told him much more, too. Before I hung up, I was told the job was Betsy's.

"I need you to get me the low-down on a woman."

"Okay. Do you got a name for me?"

"Angel Adams. Or now, wait a minute. Angel Traditor." I waited until she spelled Traditor back to me to see if she wrote it down right. I told her I thought she spelled it correctly.

"What do you want to know?"

"Everything."

"Do you have a starting place for me?"

"She has a juvenile record. Sealed, of course. I need to know what her crime was."

"I'll give it a try. But with the record sealed—"

"Anything is better than what I have now."

"You got anything else I can use? You know, like a town or city."

"Portsmouth. Whatever she did, it happened in Portsmouth."

I could hear Betsy frantically scribbling down notes. When the sound quit, I remembered something else. "Oh, and Betsy, she had a step dad. Maybe it has something to do with him. But I don't know. And her mother passed away recently. But I don't know the cause of death."

Betsy promised to start digging for answers first thing in the morning. Then we spent the next hour or so on other subjects. She told me she loved her job. Her husband was great. The baby was due in October. She was planning a trip home in July or August and would let me know as soon as she knew which month.

Then I told her I was sort of on a leave-of-absence from the paper. She thought it was a riot when I told her I had taken on the duties of an on foot paper girl. When I explained my reasons behind it, she applauded. I got more applause when I told her I hadn't taken up my former bad habit of smoking. I didn't tell her that my urges for a cigarette continued to strike on a daily basis. Or that I still used food most times to quiet those urges.

When she asked about Alicia, I told her she was about to finish her freshman year at Penn State. I did not tell her she was eloping this very weekend with a stranger to me.

I was still not ready for sleep when the long distant telephone conversation finally ended.

THIRTY-ONE

THE KITCHEN CLOCK indicated the sun should be bringing light to Saturday morning. But massive rain clouds were doing an excellent job of hiding that big ball of heat in the sky.

Despite all the caffeine that pumped a continuous flow of adrenaline to the system, I did manage to get a few hours of shut-eye during the night. I spent the last hour and twenty minutes scanning old newspapers. Stories with headlines like, *Murder comes to small town* and *Police have no suspects in the Ethel Johnson murder,* got a thorough read.

Neither story contained any new information. As a matter of fact, somebody at the paper wasn't doing their job. Where was the red strand of cheap wig hair? And why didn't they know about the lipstick found on Ethel's sleeve? God, Betsy, I miss you.

I came close to picking up the telephone and reaming a certain someone out good. But Miss Pesky reminded me of the promise I made to myself the day my lifestyle got a complete overhaul. For six months, there will be no interference whatsoever in the daily operations of the business. You will deliver papers to your customers and leave the rest to the one in charge, that inner voice repeated word for word inside my head.

The outer edge of Thursday's paper I was reading got slightly ripped when I flipped to the next page. I started to read Ethel's obituary and felt tears begin to boil over my lower eyelids. It just wasn't fair. The woman's health was excellent for a seventy-year-old. The old girl still had several good years left in her, too. Whoever took that from her deserved to be punished, severely. I'm not a diehard supporter of the death penalty. But in this case, I'd throw the switch, or give the lethal injection Pennsylvania is now using to kill off its death row inmates.

I finished the heart-sickening write up about this good and gracious woman, making a mental note of the ten o'clock scheduled funeral service. I also took special notice to the last line that said contributions could be sent to the local foster care program. That was what I'd do then, since I forgot to call and order flowers to be delivered to the funeral home.

Before I went upstairs to root around for something appropriate to wear to the service, I dug out my checkbook and wrote out a check to the foster care program. I did try Alicia's dorm again also before I finally did make my way upstairs.

THIRTY-TWO

MITCH HAD JUST FINISHED a late breakfast at the local gossip corner when I arrived around 8:45. I was dressed in all black. My big floppy hat was even black. Mitch not only looked up from the newspaper spread out in front of him, but stared at me admiringly.

"You look real nice this mornin,' Fay."

"Thank you, but I don't feel very nice," I warned as I slid into the booth across from him.

"Your ankle still givin' you fits, uh?"

"It's not my ankle."

"You look good in black," Willie complimented as she put coffee in front of me.

"Well, don't expect to see me in it again for a long, long time."

"You really aren't feelin' quite up to par," Mitch said as he and Willie exchanged bewildered looks they didn't think I saw.

"Want your usual breakfast?" Willie asked.

"No breakfast today, Willie."

There was another exchange of looks between the two of them before Willie scurried off.

"What's wrong, Fay?"

"What's right? It's still raining. I can't find my daughter. A woman who was as dear to me as my grandmother has been murdered. And Joe… Well, he has Angel now."

I looked over into sympathetic eyes. "Did I leave anything out?"

A soft smile wiggled around Mitch's mouth. I half expected to hear from him, *and you've got me.* But before his next breath, the smile was gone.

"You forgot about your ex wantin' you back," he said. "Although that could be a positive thing."

I sipped coffee while I tried to figure out if he was being a smart aleck or if he was just plain jealous. Before I could comment, and not that I was sure of what I'd say if I did, Mitch changed the subject on me. At least he steered it away from Allen and his offer for a reconciliation between us.

"Should have somethin' back from the crime lab on Ethel's clothes by Monday."

"You talking about the possible match with Angel's fingerprint?"

"Maybe. And hopefully a brand name for the lipstick found on the sleeve of Ethel's dress."

"If it's a popular brand, have fun figuring out which, among the thousands or millions of women that wear it, happened to brush lips against Ethel's sleeve."

"It's a longshot, okay. But it's somethin' besides the wig hair."

"Anything turn up on that yet?"

"None of the local beauty shops have records of recent sales in that particular shade of red."

"You check the malls? Then there's those mail order places around the country."

Mitch was starting to look as depressed as I felt when he tilted his coffee cup against his lips. He did perk up a bit when I told him I had Betsy checking into Angel's background.

THIRTY-THREE

MITCH COULDN'T BE persuaded to attend Ethel's funeral with me. So we parted company at the restaurant door with an exchange of "see you later." He attempted to dodge giant raindrops as he took off for his pickup. My hat took a slight pounding until I limped around the front of my car and dove in behind the wheel.

I was proud of myself for remembering to fish the umbrella from the trunk before I backed out of the garage at home. And it was right there on the seat next to me where I put it.

Some days I really wondered if it was worth the effort to climb out of bed. Especially days like this when I left my brain on the bed pillow. I probably could blame these occasional lapses of memory on menopause. And for all I know, that could very well be the culprit. No way was I ready to believe it was a part of growing old.

I cruised south on Front Street, past one funeral

parlor and turned into the empty parking lot of the next one. I had been afraid of being late. I looked at my wristwatch. 10:08. I was late. But the service wouldn't, couldn't, be over and done with in eight minutes. My mind may give me these occasional fits of memory loss, but I remembered what I read in the paper this morning. I was at the right funeral parlor. Besides, I just drove past another empty parking lot of the only other parlor in town. I also remembered reading the service was to be held at ten o'clock Saturday morning.

I reached for my umbrella and sent it out the door ahead of me. Just because the ankle felt strong enough to put the full weight of my body on it, didn't mean it was ready for me to sprint to the door. So I didn't.

As I climbed the steps to the door of the funeral parlor, I saw lights on inside. Before I had a chance to try the door, it opened. I recognized the handsome young man who greeted me.

"Good morning."

He was the doorman at Thomas's funeral the day before. I think he is also the undertaker's assistant.

I returned his pleasant greeting with a question. "Isn't the service for Ethel Johnson supposed to be held here?"

"Yes. But I'm afraid you missed the service."

"The paper said ten o'clock."

"Oh, yes. That would have been Thursday's paper. Yesterday's printed the correction. It was a nine o'clock service."

It must have been my heavy sigh of frustration that caused him to add, "They just left with her a short while ago. If you hurry, you might arrive at the cemetery before the preacher gives his final prayer."

I thanked him and retraced my steps to the car, although I was too steamed to step carefully and keep down the speed. Luckily, I made it inside the car without further injury to the ankle, because I felt no pain. But then, that could be because I was too busy demoting Doug Smith in my head.

Fay Cunningham is a woman of her word, I reminded myself as I slammed the car door beside me. I'll give you your six month reign as head honcho of The Susquehanna Valley Daily, as promised. But you can forget taking over on a permanent basis. This old gal is coming back.

I looked at my reflection in the rear-view mirror. A smile of determination lit up the face. The slightly pudgy one. "That is going to change too," I told my reflection in reference to the weight gain.

I fired up the Lincoln with a promise to myself. Chubby was not only going to reclaim her newspaper business, but do it at forty pounds lighter.

THIRTY-FOUR

BY THE TIME I TURNED into Harmony Cemetery, the heavy rain had slowed to a light drizzle. An assortment of old and new vehicles lined both sides of the paved road that led to the hilltop site where Ethel was apparently being buried.

My Lincoln crept up the hill. The farther it climbed, the better the view I had of the graveside mourners huddled together outside and beneath the canvas canopy.

As I reached the flat, I shifted the gearshift up into Park, but left the engine idle. At this point, the huddle was beginning to spread out. "Looks like I missed that final prayer," I said to myself.

Then I debated if I should leave the car running while I hurried over to say my final good-bye, or if I should get it out of the way so people behind me could leave. The latter of the two seemed the most sensible. The Lincoln was moving again when I spotted the empty space next to the shiny deep, blue-colored hearse. I pulled in and turned the car off. When I reached for my umbrella, I caught a side angle of Allen.

There was no doubt about it, he was aging nicely. If possible, he had grown more handsome each year. I inhaled deeply, on the verge of going off on a quick fantasy of the two of us together again. He pulled me into those powerful arms of his. Then our….

"Hey, wait a minute."

I cut the fantasy short myself. Or I should say, what I witnessed snapped me back to reality.

Angel had joined Allen. Joined *hips* with him would be more accurate. Allen was actually starting to run his hand up the backside of her tight skirt when Joe stepped into the picture.

Just because I was calling Allen every name in the book under my breath didn't mean I was going to hop out of the car and pounce on him. Not that I didn't want to. But being the mature woman I am, I decided to act the part.

By the time I did step out of the car and head in their direction, Angel was leading Joe off in another.

"Fay, I was hoping you'd show up," Allen greeted me with, along with that charming smile of his. Then his expression got serious.

"Have you heard from Alicia?"

"No. Have you?"

"Not a word. I made more calls last night. Nobody knows anything."

"Yeah, well, somebody knows something. They just aren't saying."

"Are you sure she said she was getting married? I mean, maybe you heard wrong."

"I may be getting older, Allen, but there is nothing wrong with my hearing."

I started to storm around him so I could step up to the casket that was about to be lowered into the ground. My umbrella caught the edge of his and stopped me in my tracks. Though I think his seductive tone and the words he chose next, could have had more to do with my dead stop.

"Fay, I am sorry. And I do miss you terribly."

I looked up into eyes that tried so hard to reveal sincerity. But somehow I managed to see through them. Or perhaps it was the incident I saw between he and Angel that made me see him for what he really was.

"Cut the crap, Allen. I saw you and Angel."

"Angel," he repeated with a little laugh.

"The two of you looked really cozy, real familiar together."

"Well, we are."

I knew he recognized the look I was giving him. The mean one where my eyes and mouth draw in. He immediately defended his own words with new ones.

"Not the way you're thinking. Angel worked for me for a while. She was a temp while Cherie was on maternity leave."

"Angel worked for you? When?"

He shrugged his shoulders. "I don't know. Probably a month or two ago."

"Does Joe know?"

"I guess. I don't know. Why the third degree?"

"Never mind," I told him, and was about to be on my way again when I got a glimpse of Angel and Joe. Then I took a closer look. They were down the hill from me. Their backs were to me as they stood sharing an umbrella at a fresh grave.

I looked away when Angel looked over her shoulder, directly up at Allen and me. There was another reason I looked away so quickly, other than not wanting her to catch me staring. Even from this distance, which was several yards, her eyes belonged to that same soulless creature I had seen before.

"It's great about Joe and her," Allen was saying,

as I tried to chase out the eerie feeling that crept down inside of me. "Joe is playing the part of the proud papa who has just been told he has a daughter."

"How long have you known about Angel being Joe's daughter?"

"Joe told me today."

THIRTY-FIVE

ONCE I SAID A FEW WORDS over Ethel's casket and started for my car in tears, the cemetery was nearly deserted. Deserted of those among the living, that is. Allen was gone. So was Angel and Joe.

I started to get into my car, but changed my mind. I thought I should have a look at the fresh grave Angel and Joe visited, even though I was certain it belonged to Thomas. My mind was so polluted with unanswered questions that I could feel an approaching migraine.

For starters, I was mad at myself again. I was getting old. What else explained the absence of the once admired quick thinking puzzle solver I'd been known for. I should have figured something wasn't right the minute Joe told me Angel was his daughter. Because by then, Mitch had already told me Angel lived on North Front Street a few months before taking up residence at Joe's. If she'd been in town all that time, how come it took so long to tell Joe he was, as Allen had put it, a papa?

When I stepped up to Thomas's gravesite, another question I had forgotten about returned. What was Angel doing at Thomas's funeral yesterday? That question alone was responsible for piling on a half dozen more.

By the time I staggered back up the hill to my car, my head felt like it was about to explode. I rooted around in the glove compartment for the bottle of pain killers I had stashed in there for emergencies like this one. I found the bottle and popped three of the pills in my mouth and swallowed them without the benefit of water.

As I was stuffing the bottle back inside the glove compartment, the opened pack of cigarettes fell out onto the floor. I eyed them for several seconds before I closed the compartment door. I picked up the pack of smokes and tossed them out the window next to me. A decision had been reached. It was now or never. I had chosen now. And in doing so, was perfectly willing to cough up the three hundred dollar fine for littering if I was caught breaking the law.

THIRTY-SIX

My STOMACH WAS HOLLERING for food, but I wasn't ready to answer it. I had a stronger need that was going to be satisfied first. Thanks to Allen, I had missed my opportunity to speak to Joe at the cemetery, to offer sincere condolences. The words were said yesterday, but they should be repeated on the day Ethel was laid to rest. I wouldn't blame Joe if he didn't allow me inside his house after I missed the service. In my eyes, there was no excuse for my tardiness. It would be easy to blame the paper for the misprint, but I should have double-checked with someone.

THE HEAVIER RAIN had returned by the time I parked behind Joe's deteriorating mansion. I knew why he didn't hire a contractor to do the necessary repairs on the house. Of the two brothers, Joe was the hoarder. It would be nicer to say he was the conservative one of the two. But the truth is, he pinched every penny. And this man had millions to pinch. The only reason he owned the mansion and Mercedes was because he bought them at a bankruptcy auction for a song.

Joe was born in Naples, Italy. He and his brother landed in New York City at the age of eighteen and nineteen. Joe the oldest of the two. They had opened a small pizza parlor there. Before long, the one parlor became two, then three. In a few years, they had a chain stretching along the New Jersey coast line. Then they moved westward and landed in Pennsylvania.

It was after they set up housekeeping in Milton that something happened between them; something so terrible they became bitter enemies. Joe never told me what caused this family feud that survived all these years. Twenty-some, to be more exact. The brothers were in their late forties when the feud began.

Thomas liked the ladies too much to ever commit to just one by getting married. Whereas Joe was too busy building his pizza empire to take the necessary time to build a loving relationship with a woman. At least until Ethel had come into his life.

But there must have been another woman before Ethel. I strongly doubted Angel was conceived during a one-night fling. As I said, since I've known Joe, I've known a real miser. Whereas Thomas liked to throw his money around. Or more correctly, Thomas liked to flaunt his wealth. A flashy new luxury car every year, a new house every other. He even had his own private tailor moved here from overseas somewhere. I believe it was Italy. Joe, on the other hand, was content shopping at your regular guy department store. He always looked neat, though. White shirts starched as stiff as a board. A coat and tie worn regularly when he left the house. At home, the attire is much more casual. But then, it would look a little more than eccentric to mow the lawn and tend the garden in a suit and tie.

Joe still did his own yard work. I believe this was because he enjoyed it so much, not because he was too tight to pay a neighbor kid twenty bucks to cut the grass.

The one extravagance Joe allowed himself was a full-time housekeeper. Ethel had a tiny apartment in town where she slept. But from daybreak to nightfall, six days a week, she was at Joe's house, or off somewhere with him. Sundays were reserved for her sister and her large family; the family Ethel never had. By her own terms, Ethel had considered herself an old maid.

THIRTY-SEVEN

I GRABBED MY UMBRELLA and braced myself for the downpour I was about to step into as I headed for Joe's back door. The screen door Joe hooked onto the kitchen door frame every spring, and took off every fall, had appeared since my last visit.

I tossed my umbrella to a corner of the porch. Then I reached up to knock on the wood frame, but didn't. Through a dusty screen, I saw Joe sitting at the table. His back was to me, but I could tell he was crying.

"Joe," I called softly.

I repeated his name a second time before I started to let myself inside. The door squeaked on its rusty hinges and Joe jerked around.

"Hi, there," I said, trying to smile, but wanting to cry with him.

He turned his back to me again. I'm not sure if it was to dry his eyes or if he really was upset with me for missing the service. I pulled out the table chair next to him and slowly let myself down on it. Joe was still dabbing at his eyes with his handkerchief, which allowed me to breathe a little easier.

The words I wanted to say refused to come right away. So I reached over for his hand. When he gave mine a squeeze, I knew I was off the hook. He wasn't mad at me.

"I'm sorry I missed you at the cemetery. I arrived late. By the time I finished saying good-bye to Ethel, Angel and you had left Thomas's grave side."

Joe looked over at me through watery eyes. My hand was squeezed a little tighter.

"I told Thomas I forgave him."

"That's good, Joe."

He shook his head yes. Then he looked straight over into my eyes that were also watery. "Angel didn't think I should do it. Said she wouldn't. Couldn't."

"Where is Angel?" I asked, while I tried to understand why Angel would tell him such a thing.

"Off somewhere in the woods."

"Joe, it's raining buckets out there."

"Says she likes the rain."

"Well what's she doing in the woods?"

"Goes there to think. Says she's been in 'bout all the woods 'round here."

Never mind that I thought sitting in the woods in

the middle of a rainstorm was a bit off the wall, it was the other part Joe said that was giving my head fits. The part about Angel being in all the woods in the area.

"She'll be along soon if she's anything like her mother. Marie did her best thinking out in the wild, too."

"That's interesting," I said before swallowing long and hard.

"I flew out there to Ohio, you know. Stood over her grave and told her I forgave her, too."

"You mean that's where you were on this trip you just took? You flew to Ohio?"

Joe affirmed with a nod. "I loved that woman, Fay. Marie was that once in a lifetime love they write those romance books about."

He looked away from me and pounded his fist down hard on the tabletop.

"I'd have married her, too, if it weren't for that scoundrel brother of mine."

I finally knew. It was a woman that turned brother against brother all those years ago. But I remained silent so Joe could continue telling his story.

"He run off with her. When she told him she was carrying his child, he left her."

"How do you know this? I mean, that she was pregnant?"

"I read it in her diary Angel gave me. She wrote in there that I fathered the child. That's why Thomas didn't do the right thing and marry her. He knew the baby was mine."

"But why didn't Marie tell you? Why did she run off with Thomas when it was your baby she was carrying?"

The screen door squeaked open before Joe had a chance to answer. But the look he had been giving me before Angel came in the door, told me he didn't know the answer.

I watched Angel bend over and kiss Joe on the cheek before starting to take off rain gear. And in the process, she said to me, "Hello, Fay. It was very nice of you to stop by and keep Father company while I was out."

"Well, I didn't get a chance to talk to him at the cemetery."

"Were you there? I didn't see you."

I watched her strike one of those long matches on the side of its box again before putting it to the gas on the front burner of Joe's old stove. All the while I was biting my tongue to keep from calling her a liar. She did see me at the cemetery. Our eyes met long enough for me to revisit that spooky place deep inside her.

"I'm going to heat Father and I soup. Would you like some, Fay?"

"No," I answered immediately. Then I jumped up saying, "I have some things to do. But I would like to use the bathroom before I go, if that's okay?"

I expected Angel to be first to politely give me permission. But instead, she guided the can of soup against the cutting edge of the electric can opener while Joe spoke.

"You know you don't need permission. Just go."

I scooted out of the kitchen like I had to go real bad. The truth is, I had no plans to use the toilet.

THIRTY-EIGHT

I KNEW EXACTLY WHERE I was going and it wasn't into the bathroom. The night I searched the house for Joe when I didn't believe Angel after she said he wasn't home, I discovered which of the several guest rooms Angel had laid claim to.

Lucky for me, she chose one of the rooms next to the bathroom at the top of the stairs. I quickly and quietly opened the closed bedroom door after I remembered to close the bathroom door. My thinking cap continued to work at top speed like it used to, when it reminded me to close the bedroom door behind me, too. With any luck, it would continue to work with me. Perhaps even tell me exactly what it was I was looking for.

Catching Angel in an outright lie is what gave me the idea to have a closer look inside her bedroom. The room was tidy. No clutter. No dust. Nothing much in the way of personal treasures brought from home. The only way I knew I was in the right room was because I saw skinny clothes hanging in the closet the night I searched the house.

Quietly, I began pulling out dresser drawers. Undergarments were neatly folded and spread out enough that I could see it was pointless to waste time carefully lifting bras and panties to check underneath. The rest of the drawers were the same way. I took a minute to let my eyes sweep over the room, while I asked myself where, among the few pieces of furniture, I might find something.

My eyes steadied on the full-sized brass bed. I was smiling as I hurried over to it and began lifting corners of the mattress. Under the third corner, I found it. Or something. When I pulled out what looked like an old hardbound address book, I thought I heard someone on the stairs.

I held my breath and listened. All was quiet. Then I hoisted up my dress and stuck the book down the front of my panty hose. It was risky to press my luck by not leaving while the coast was still clear, but I just couldn't resist taking another look inside the closet.

The door creaked as I started to pull it open. I paused, then moved it a little more. There was no light inside, which made it very difficult to see much more than clothes and shoe boxes hanging over the edge of the shelf above the clothes rack. My eyes strained hard against the near darkness. When I looked toward the one end, a different shaped box stood out.

"A wig box," I said aloud in answer to my own question of what kind of box it was.

I started to reach up for it when behind me I heard, "Fay, everything all right up there?"

A ball of fear landed in my throat, temporarily cutting off my breath. I tiptoed over to the bedroom door. I knew I was taking a big chance opening the door a crack. If Angel was standing at the foot of the stairs, she'd see me. But I really didn't have a choice.

When one eye peeked through the crack, it saw the coast was clear. So this old gal wasted no time slipping out into the hall and into the bathroom. I flushed the toilet, remembering the sound of the toilet water draining down the pipes can be heard in the kitchen. Then I took a quick look in the mirror that was attached to the back of the bathroom door. The little book I had tucked in my panty hose didn't jut out from my loosely fitted dress from any angle I checked.

I was at the bottom of the steps before I remembered I forgot to close the closet door. Should I go back up or not?

"There you are," Angel said as she posed in the kitchen and hall doorway.

"What a relief," I said, my hand going to my stomach and touching the book as I started toward her. I said a quick good-bye to Joe with a promise to stop by the next day, then I headed for the door.

"You take good care of him now, Angel" is how I bid farewell to the meticulous young woman who glared threateningly from that hall and kitchen archway.

I probably never will know why Angel kept her bedroom, and self, spic-and-span clean, but didn't dirty her hands with the rest of the house. Of all things, that is what I was thinking when I drove off.

THIRTY-NINE

I PULLED INTO THE EMPTY space next to Mitch's pickup parked outside the local gossip corner. Once I had my car turned off, I took a good look around me. The coast was clear. And this old gal's curiosity refused to allow me to take the extra minutes it would mean to lock myself inside the ladies' room before I hiked the bottom part of my dress up the thighs.

I continued to keep a close watch around me as my hand wormed its way up the front of my panty hose until I had hold of the little book. I quickly flipped back the cover and leafed through pages. They were not pages filled with addresses and telephone numbers like I had thought. I had in my hands the diary of one Marie Adams Traditor.

For one mouth-drying moment, I considered what I was about to do. It's not that I wasn't accustomed to invading people's privacy. I'm a newspaper publisher, after all. But it almost seemed sacrilege to read someone's personal diary without their permission. *You can't get permission from a dead woman,* that inner voice reminded me.

I know that still didn't give me the right to read Marie's diary. But since she was no longer with us, I didn't feel quite so guilty.

As I started to scan down the first page, I did it in hopes of reading things differently than Joe had. Maybe he missed the part that explained why Marie took up with Thomas when she was carrying Joe's baby. Before I got past the first paragraph of neatly written longhand, I was interrupted by the tap on my door window.

I saw the cowboy hat before I saw Mitch's weatherbeaten face. He had to have seen what I was doing. He wouldn't know what I was reading, but I still closed the book and shoved it under my seat before I hit the window button.

"Everything okay?" he ask as the window slid down.

"You're getting wet" is how I answered.

"Was just about to take off, but I've got time for another cup a coffee."

"You mean you haven't downed your limit for the day yet?"

Mitch snickered. "I'm weeks ahead of my two-cup-a-day limit."

I understood. Or thought I did. The man who had held fast to this nutrition kick he was on for the last several months was backsliding. And in his case, I thought it was an asset. He had grown way too uptight to suit me. First it was the pepperoni pizza and soda, and now the extra doses of caffeine to the system. Then again, maybe he was backsliding too much, too fast. If he wasn't careful, he might just flip open a can of beer before the weekend was through.

He held the door for me while I worked myself out of the front seat and into the rain. Not the heavy stuff like earlier, but it was still coming down enough that it wouldn't take long to get soaked. Mitch left his hat and rain coat on the rack inside the entrance door. I left the floppy black hat on my head.

When Willie stopped by our booth to take my order, I told her I was back to the midday rabbit food Mitch was so hooked on these days. At least I *thought* he still was.

I watched her jot down salad on her order pad and quickly said water when she started to write coffee. Mitch didn't say a word about what I ordered. But I could tell by the way he was looking at me, he was happily surprised. Maybe a bit confused as well.

FORTY

I WASN'T GOING TO TELL Mitch, but it sort of slipped
out about the diary I stole from Angel's bedroom.
This, of course, was after I told him everything that
led up to, and played a part in my decision to
become a thief. I didn't mention the fact that in my
hurry to leave Angel's bedroom, I forgot to close the
closet door that had been shut when I entered the
room. Then again, I didn't say anything about the
box I saw that resembled those used to store wigs
in, either. There was also a slip of memory about
what a meticulous person Angel is and would surely
know I was inside her bedroom when she saw the
closet door standing open.

According to Mitch, there was a simple explanation for Angel's appearance at Thomas's funeral.
The man was her uncle, after all. So why wouldn't
she attend his funeral.

"So how come if she's the grieving niece, she

didn't think Joe should forgive Thomas? Angel couldn't. But why?"

Then again, maybe she attended the service and was the one who actually did spit on Thomas, that inner voice suggested before Mitch answered verbally.

"She resented Thomas because he kept her mother from marryin' Joe," I said as I chewed tasteless lettuce. "I mean, you're the one who said Angel had a drunkin' bum for a stepdad. If it wouldn't a been for Thomas's interference, she'd a had a dear, sweet old Joe all those years she was growin' up. And why didn't Marie ever tell Joe he was Angel's father?" I let him stew on that while I took another big bite of leafy vegetables.

"Maybe she figured Joe wouldn't believe her after she'd been with Thomas. Or maybe she didn't know which brother really was the kid's father."

"Now that sounds closer to the truth," I said. Then another thought popped into my head. "What if Thomas was Angel's father? I mean, think about it."

Mitch did for about one second.

"Sounds like you may have somethin' there."

I thought so, too. Until I remembered the diary. Joe had said he read in there that he was Angel's father. This information was shared with Mitch.

Then I wolfed down the remainder of my salad so I could hurry home and read the little book without any interruptions.

Mitch didn't ask if it would be okay, or if I planned to be home. He just said he'd stop by the house later. Then we went our separate ways. I'm not sure where he was going. But this old gal was going straight home to read.

FORTY-ONE

I WALKED IN THE DOOR at home to a hungry feline. When I reached up in the cupboard for a can of cat food, I noticed the blinking light on the answering machine. I hit the message button, holding my breath Alicia had called. By the time the tape rewound, I had Kitty's food opened. As I spooned out the fishy smelling stuff, I heard Betsy's voice.

"Fay, it's Betsy. Drop everything and give me a ring when you get in."

I heard a second caller hang up without leaving a message. Then while the tape returned to its start position, I tapped out Betsy's home number I had written down in the back of my telephone book. After three rings, her answering machine kicked on. "Betsy, if you're there, pick up. It's Fay."

I waited a few seconds to the sound of silence. "Okay, so you're not home. I am, and will stay here until you call."

Before I headed for my favorite spot to curl up

on and decipher the contents of Marie's diary, I called Alicia's dorm. Like numerous times before, I listened to a number of unanswered rings and finally hung up. I thought about giving Allen a jingle, but decided against it. If he had heard from our daughter, he would have called. He would have left a message since I wasn't home.

"If you want to join me, I'll be in the living room," I told Kitty, who was too busy chowing down to pay me any attention. Then I picked up the diary I dropped on the counter when I came in and headed for that comfortable spot on the corner of the living room couch. Instead of propping my foot on the coffee table, I kicked off my loafers and tucked both feet up underneath me. It would have been a good idea to ice down the ankle since there was still some swelling, but I didn't want to take the time to mess with it. My mind was hungry for answers this little book possibly held.

I was several pages into Marie's diary when I knew something was terribly wrong. The fact that tears were rolling down my cheeks confirmed what Joe said earlier. I read about one of those once in a lifetime romances. It was just as he had said. Only the pages I read never mentioned Joe as the father to the baby Marie carried. The pages I read told about how Marie had met Thomas. They had a brief affair that lasted until the day Thomas introduced his older brother Joe to her. It was love at first sight for Marie. She soon discovered Joe felt the same way. Life was magical for nearly a month.

The doctor told Marie it wasn't the virus going around that had her hanging her head over the toilet every morning for the last week. She was pregnant. Marie was elated, until the doctor told her how far along she was.

She was devastated by the news. The doctor offered the name of a clinic in New York that performed abortions, since it was still illegal to have one in Pennsylvania. Marie had no money for an abortion. But even if she did, she would not be able to go through with it. She had conceived a child out of wedlock. She would not compound that sin by adding another.

She loved Joe too much to deceive him by telling him she was carrying his baby. When she confronted Thomas, he told her they would run off and get married. Start fresh in another state. Then Thomas drove her to an abortion clinic out of state, gave her a fistful of hundred dollar bills, and left her at the door.

Marie was alone in a strange city. But she had enough money to catch a bus to about anywhere she wanted to go. So that's what she did. She took a bus to Ohio where an old girlfriend from high school had settled.

The diary ended with the birth of Angel. But nowhere from beginning to end had I read that Joe had fathered Marie's child.

FORTY-TWO

I CLOSED THE LITTLE book and left it on the couch and headed upstairs to finally get out of the dress and panty hose. My brain was tossing things around the entire time I showered and pulled on a sweatsuit. There was only one possible solution to the question that had been giving me fits. The question of where Joe read that he was Angel's father. Joe had to have read a completely different version of the one I read. A forged diary. Joe read the one Angel wrote. I had the original, the one that contained the truth.

But why had Angel gone to the trouble of forgery? Why didn't she just confront Thomas?

"Maybe she did," I was saying when the telephone rang.

I was on my way down the steps and picked up in the kitchen after the third ring.

"Fay, it's Francie."

"Francie," I repeated, surprised.

"Sounds like you were expectin' someone else."

I was. Betsy. But I didn't say so. "What's up?" is what I said.

"You better get out a there real fast."

"What?"

"The state boys are with the judge right now. Gettin' 'em a warrant to search your house. You hear me, girl? They're comin' for you."

"Who's coming for me?"

"The police. They got 'em a tip that you're the one that done Ethel."

"Me?"

"Got a go," came in a rush before I heard the click of the receiver being put down.

I have no idea why, but I grabbed my car keys and wallet off the counter and took off for the garage. I was on the road before I realized what I was doing. Or at least I thought I knew. I was running from the law—and driving like crazy straight *to* the law. I guess I should say, the *former* law. Mitch was no longer an officer of the law.

The pot-holed private lane to his small farm outside of town was long and narrow. Once I spotted the farmhouse, I looked around for Mitch's pickup. I didn't see it anywhere as I parked in front of the house. I knew he didn't plan on being out late or else he would have left the porch light on. With the clouds and rain, darkness was going to arrive early. Probably within the next hour.

So I would sit and wait for Mitch to return. It would also give me a chance to put some sense into what was happening. Or more like, what was *about* to happen. I could almost see handcuffs slapped on my wrists before I was hauled off to the slammer. Nobody would listen to my cries of innocence that are heard far and wide from convicts daily.

But it was true. I was innocent. I didn't kill Ethel. I couldn't kill a soul. Well, I suppose if it was me or the other guy, I'd defend myself. But why on earth would I want to do in Ethel Johnson? And just who put the cops onto me?

That question was easily answered. Angel had discovered I was snooping in her bedroom. Perhaps she knew the diary was gone too. I was onto her, and she had to do something about it fast. Before I had a chance to show Joe the diary I had stolen. The original. Francie said the police were getting a search warrant for my house. But what were they expecting to find? There was nothing there to link me to Ethel's murder.

So how come you didn't stick around to watch them turn up nothing? Miss Pesky wanted answered. At first, I didn't have one. But it didn't take long to figure out I just plain panicked.

FORTY-THREE

I EYED THE GLOVE compartment for longer than I care to say before I remembered the cigarettes were no longer in there. Without them there, the urge for one passed quicker than on previous occasions. But something in the way of food to nibble on while I waited for Mitch to return home would have made the wait more bearable.

No smokes, no food, meant I had to settle for something much less soothing to my jittery nerves. I pulled down the visor and reached for the pen clipped fast to a corner. I went from twirling it through my fingers to chewing on the end of it while I played the question and answer game inside my head.

I was positive Angel set me up to take the fall for Ethel's murder. I also had myself talked into believing she was the one who committed the heinous act. What I couldn't figure out was why she had done it. Mitch may have something with his theory that she wanted Joe all to herself. But that meant she'd have to start knocking off people regularly. I admit Joe had become sort of a recluse the last couple of years since his retirement, but there were a number of people who remained in his circle of friends. I was probably closest to him next to Ethel. Then there was Alicia—

My God, no. Was it possible? Did Angel have something to do with my daughter's sudden disappearance? Was this elopement thing just a smoke screen? "You go near my daughter and I'll strangle you with my bare hands," I vowed to the image of Angel that loomed in my thoughts.

The fingers and mouth gave the pen one heck of a workout before my anger was brought down to a level that made me see I had let the imagination get the best of me. It was Alicia's voice I heard on my answering machine, after all. It was Alicia who said she couldn't come home this weekend because she was getting married.

By the time I calmed myself down with this piece of analysis, a set of headlights flashed into the car. For a minute there, fear gripped me by the throat. What if it's the police? They found my hiding place and had come to haul me off to jail. Or worse yet, what if it's Angel, come to do me in like she had Ethel?

There was still enough light in the day for me to see it was Mitch's pint-sized truck pulling in next to my Lincoln.

FORTY-FOUR

THERE WAS NO TAP ON my car window. No wait for permission to join me inside. Mitch just opened the passenger side door and slid in on the seat next to me.

"I really should remember to start locking my doors," I said.

"I believe you ran a newspaper story about that not so long ago."

"Sure did. Ran it after car jacking became so popular."

Then came the silence. Mitch was swinging his cowboy hat in front of his knees, his head was down so he was watching his fingers reshape the rim. While I impatiently waited for him to tell me what was eating at him so I could tell him I was running from the law.

"Fay," he finally began, "the police want a talk to you." He peeked over at me before looking straight ahead at the wet windshield. "They was over at your place when I stopped by a little while ago."

When he looked over at me a second time, our eyes fixed and held. "They found a red wig out back in your garbage can."

"Damn," I cursed and slapped the steering wheel.

Mitch's eyes widened. His expression filled with surprise and disbelief. "You already knew?"

I exhaled deeply. "Francie tipped me off the police were on their way. The wig is news."

It only seemed fair it was Mitch's turn to become angry. "So you just take off and make a run for it like someone guilty would do?"

"You know I didn't kill Ethel. Angel set me up."

"Thought you said she wasn't no killer?"

"I was wrong, okay. But your jealousy motive just doesn't make sense."

"So why'd she do it then?"

"I don't know."

"Okay. So why set you up?"

"That's the easy part. She knows I searched her bedroom. The diary's gone. And it's a different diary than the one Joe read. The one I have says Thomas is Angel's papa. My guess is, Angel wrote her own version from the original. Joe was given a little book of fiction. I'm also thinking the birth certificate

Angel told me about finding in her mother's safety deposit box was doctored."

"Or else she had a fake one printed up. They're not that difficult to come by."

"Right. Then there's the wig box I saw in Angel's bedroom closet."

"You didn't tell me about a wig box."

"Well, I'm not positive that's what it was. I didn't have time to take a look inside."

Another stretch of silence; a necessary break to give us both time to think about the things we just said.

Mitch broke the silence. "You can bet that box isn't in her closet anymore."

"And the wig that was in it just happened to be disposed of in my garbage can."

"Then she makes an anonymous call to the police. Tips them off to where they can find the wig too."

"Wait a minute. The paper didn't print the part about red wig hair found at the crime scene. So how would Angel have known how desperate the police were to find the owner of the wig? Only the killer would know how important the fake hair could be to cracking the case."

My bubble wasn't popped because Mitch didn't

share my sudden enthusiasm. But it burst when he spoke again.

"This mornin's paper had the story on the front page. Even included the part about the lipstick smears found on Ethel's dress sleeve. The story ended by sayin' the evidence was shipped off to the crime lab in Harrisburg for analysis."

If it wouldn't be so hypocritical, I probably would have cursed the paper for suddenly doing its job too well. And without the benefit of my carefully guided influence.

FORTY-FIVE

MITCH CONVINCED ME it would look better to a judge if I turned myself in should it become necessary to stand before one to ask to be released on bail; which is not a requirement when the accused is charged with murder.

I agreed to follow Mitch to the state police barracks, where it was highly likely I'd be charged with murder. If not today, then on another day in the very near future.

Allen was called from Mitch's farmhouse before our too short a drive to the police barracks. I never expected to find Allen home on a Saturday night. Especially now that he was a swinging bachelor again. But he was home; he'd been on the telephone trying to track down our daughter the entire evening. So I was told.

Once he recognized my voice, he thought I was calling with news of Alicia. When I told him I required his legal services, I'm sure I heard him drop the phone after he was told I was a suspect in the murder of Ethel Johnson. I could read his thoughts without even seeing his face. I just blew those political aspirations of his.

I assured him I did not kill Ethel before he agreed to meet me at the barracks outside of town. In the event I arrived there before he did, I was told to say nothing, answer no questions.

MITCH HELD the glass door for me to enter the one-story brick building first. He motioned for me to have a seat on one of the two plastic chairs in the dinky waiting area. I was too nervous to sit down. So I hovered behind Mitch as he stepped up to the glass window.

"How's it goin,' Fred?" Mitch said to the uniformed trooper on the other side of the glass.

"Be a lot better after next week. Come Friday, I'm hangin' it up like you did."

"Well, take it from me, this early retirement stuff ain't all it's cracked up to be."

That was news to me. I was under the impression Mitch loved his new role of little organic farmer.

"Is Lewis here?" I heard Mitch finally say after their brief exchange of catch up.

"Yeah, he's back there. But look out, he's in a

real foul mood tonight. That murder case, you know."

I shrank behind Mitch after Fred's last words. I think I expected him to suddenly recognize me from a mug shot that was being circulated. Even though down deep inside me I knew that wasn't so. Or I didn't think it was.

Mitch led the way through the all wood door and down a dark dreary hallway with mostly closed doors lining both sides. The door at the end of the hall was opened. A male voice was shouting words I choose not to repeat. I watched Mitch throw up his hand in sort of a hello salute to the man standing behind a cluttered desk, cigarette hanging from his lips, as he hollered into the phone. When his eyes looked beyond Mitch to me, he hung up on whoever he was bawling out.

I was trembling before the giant went silent. When his voice came again, only much softer, my knees still knocked together.

"How's it goin', Mitch," the giant said as he smashed out his cigarette in the overflowing ashtray on his desk.

"Lewis," Mitch began, sliding an arm around me and nudging me out into the open, "this is Fay Cunningham. The lady your boys wanted to have a chat with."

After the longest second in my life of being scrutinized by a pair of unnerving dark eyes, I was given the complete title and name of this brute who wore a shirt and tie.

"I'm Lieutenant Lewis Evans, Mrs. Cunningham. Do you want to have a seat."

His words may have come in the form of a question, but they were said more in the way of an order.

Mitch cleared magazines from a metal folding chair for me to sit down on. I did, while the two men worked their way toward the only door out of the room. The big guy broke from whatever he was whispering to Mitch long enough to tell me they'd be right back.

They no sooner left me alone with my bundled up nerves, and Allen shot into the room.

"My God, Fay, how did this happen? You didn't tell them anything, did you?"

Anger was giving my nerves a temporary reprieve as I watched this man I once loved more than life, begin to prance around me like he did that day he told me he wanted a divorce. Only this day, I wasn't an emotional wreck, crying my eyes out.

It must have been the mean way I was looking at him that brought him to his senses. Because before I could say a word, the prancing seized, and he cleared off a chair and collapsed on it.

"I'm sorry, Fay. You okay?"

"What do you think? I'm about to be charged with murder. But hey, I'm just Jim Dandy."

"I said I was sorry."

Our eyes exchanged these looks that said apology was accepted. Time to get on with the important business at hand.

"On the phone you said they searched the house. Did they find anything?"

"They pulled a red wig out of the garbage can."

"Jesus, Fay. Do you know what this means? I mean, all they got a do is match it with the hair found in Ethel's hand and...."

He was on his feet again, pacing in this small circle. His head was down, one hand on a hip. "You're gonna need a lawyer."

"That's why I called you."

"No. You're gonna need a criminal lawyer. I handle mostly deed transfers, wills, and divorces."

"I didn't kill her, Allen. The wig was put in my garbage by the real killer."

He stood still, his eyes wide as he looked down at me. That's when I noticed he missed a shirt button when he was dressing in his usual lawyer attire of suit and tie.

Mitch and his big buddy returned before I had the

opportunity to tell Allen to fix his crooked shirt. Or to ask if it mattered the killer might be coming after me.

Handshakes were exchanged between Allen and Lewis, along with names and titles. Hands were not gripped and shook between Allen and Mitch. Each acknowledged the other with a quick, and forced nod. Then it came time for the serious stuff.

"Either you're gonna book her, or we're out of here," Allen said before Evans got all the way around his desk to the chair he was headed for.

"Your client came here voluntarily."

I could see Mitch was about to jump in, but since I was being talked about like I was not in the same room with the three of them, I thought it only fair I remind them.

"He's right, Allen. I came here to tell them I didn't kill Ethel Johnson," I said, looking directly up into the Lieutenant's intense eyes.

"And with that said, I guess I have to repeat my lawyer's words. You either charge me or I go home."

FORTY-SIX

Mitch followed me home. Allen offered to, but was told his services were no longer needed for the night.

It wasn't until Mitch and I sat at my kitchen table sipping coffee that I was reminded, come Monday I could expect to need those lawyer services again. The only reason I wasn't booked for Ethel's murder yet, was because the strand of hair found wrapped around Ethel's fingers was at the crime lab.

The wig found in my garbage would have to be sent down to see if they had a match. If they did, Fay Cunningham was in serious trouble.

"So I have until Monday then," I repeated as I got up to refill our mugs.

"Unless we can prove the wig was a plant. And that's not gonna be easy."

"Or prove Angel is the real killer," I said, and sat

my Mr. Coffee pot back on its burner and reached for the telephone.

"Who you callin' at this hour?" Mitch asked.

"Betsy. She found something out about Angel. Only problem is, we keep getting each other's answering machines," I told him as I hung up on the sound of Betsy's recorded message.

We finished our coffee. How I was going to break the news about the diary to Joe was discussed a little in the process. Although neither one of us knew quite how to approach him on the subject. But he had to be told. He had to be given the book to read so he'd have the proof to back up my words when I told him Angel was not his daughter.

Then there was the possibility Angel would convince Joe the copy I presented him was the forgery. We weren't sure how that would be handled should it occur. Which we were certain would.

We had the night ahead to sleep on it, though. Maybe by morning we'd have that problem figured out. Maybe by morning I'd hear from Betsy and have some background information on Angel that would help solve a lot of things.

Mitch left somewhere around eleven. I locked up the house as he had instructed twice before I walked him to the door.

Then I headed upstairs for bed. I needed sleep, a chance to recharge the batteries for what promised to be a difficult day ahead of me.

FORTY-SEVEN

THE DIGITAL CLOCK ON the night stand read 2:11 a.m. when I grumbled a hello into the telephone.

"Fay, Betsy here. Sorry about waking you, but I just got home from the hospital."

By this time I had the night stand light on and was sitting on the edge of my bed.

"You okay?"

"I'm a basket case. My mother-in-law had a heart attack. We've been at the hospital most of the afternoon and night."

"She's gonna be okay though, right?"

Silence on Betsy's end. And I was certain I heard her start to cry.

"Bets."

"She passed away a short while ago, Fay."

"Oh, no."

I paused a minute until this sick feeling finished squirming its way out of my stomach and up to the throat. If I swallowed, I was afraid I'd suffer a reverse attack. So I opened my mouth instead so it could escape.

"What can I do?" I finally asked.

"I'll let you know when the shock wears off," she said as she sniffed back tears.

"How's the baby?"

I could almost see her reach for her stomach and begin to massage the fetus growing inside. I could also tell by her tone it was wise on my part to change the subject.

"The little stinker's growing like a weed. You should see the size of me already."

"Can't wait."

Then there was another shorter stretch of silence before Betsy said, "Fay, I called earlier to warn you. This Angel girl is a real sicko."

"I think I'm beginning to figure that out."

"She's spent time in a mental institution. But that's only the half of it. She was first evaluated at the ripe old age of nine."

"Nine! My God, what did she do?"

"Accidentally locked her stepdaddy in an abandoned refrigerator in the woods behind their house. And get this, it took her three days to tell someone."

The minute she mentioned the refrigerator, I was thinking about Ethel. I was one hundred percent certain now that Angel was the one who stuffed poor Ethel in the refrigerator at a local dump site in the woods. I told Betsy as much. I told her the whole story about Ethel, about the diary. I even included the part about my visit to the police because I had become their number one suspect in the murder.

Again, Betsy returned to the incident surrounding Angel's stepfather's death. And how she got away with what was clearly murder.

"She told the police she and her daddy were playing hide-n-seek in the woods. She saw her daddy hide in the refrigerator. He left the door open a crack, so he could peek out and watch for her. But Angel tricked him and snuck up from behind and shut the door."

"Yeah, but a nine-year-old probably wouldn't know he couldn't get out of there on his own."

"Exactly how she got away with it. When she was questioned, she said she thought her daddy got out. The reason he hadn't come home was because he was off on one of those trips he often took.

"He was a lush, Fay. And Angel's mother confirmed the fact that he'd go off for days at a time on drinking binges. By day three, Angel just happened to mention to her mother about the game they had been playing that last day she saw him. And about how she shut the refrigerator door."

"What you're telling me does sound very believable."

"A few years later, when she ended up in the state hospital after attempting suicide, her therapist got the shock of her life when Angel told her the story about how she shut her stepdaddy in the refrigerator."

"She told her she did it intentionally?"

"Oh, yeah. She knew there was no way he could get out of there once she closed the door. And get this, she knew that because her stepdaddy used to lock her in there when she was a bad little girl. He'd open the door in time to keep her from suffocating."

"That's awful."

So awful that I suddenly felt sorry for Angel.

"That's not all. He abused her sexually, Fay. The first time was through the night. He held her bed pillow over her face so she wouldn't scream. She lost consciousness before he finished with her."

I found myself hating a man I had never met. He deserved to be shut in that refrigerator. Poor Angel. Clever Angel.

"During Angel's stay at the mental hospital, she tried to smother another patient with her bed pillow. Would have got away with it too, if an orderly hadn't come along.

"That's how she ended up with the criminal record. She was charged with attempted murder. Served a few years in a juvenile detention center and was released. The records were sealed because of her age. Little Angel was offered a fresh start in the world."

"This is all so incredible," I sighed as I attempted to absorb it all.

"It's also very confidential. None of it can be used to help prove she murdered your friend Ethel, Fay."

"But we're talking about a very dangerous young woman here," I reminded in protest.

"You don't have to tell me that. I was afraid to go to sleep after hearing the story."

"Just where did you hear the story?"

"You know I never reveal my sources, Fay. But I will say it came from someone who was there. A few files were accidentally dropped in my lap too."

"You have to send them to me, Betsy."

"Can't do. They've already been returned, as promised."

We talked a while longer before the long distance conversation ended.

"Be careful, Fay" were Betsy's last words to me.

FORTY-EIGHT

IT WAS AFTER THREE in the morning when we hung up. And this old gal was too wound up to consider going back to sleep. I thought about calling Mitch so I could relay the incredible story I'd just been told. But since that's all it was, and there was no way it could be used by the police, I decided against waking him. It would be light out in a couple of hours. I'd wait until then. Until I knew he'd be getting up.

The next problem was how I was going to spend those hours that stretched in front of me. I headed downstairs to put on a fresh pot of coffee. The ankle had stiffened up on me the short time I'd spent in bed, but once I started moving around on it, it loosened up enough that I forgot about it for the time being. Or at least until I carried a fresh cup of coffee into the living room with me and saw the set of crutches propped up against the one end of the couch.

I'd put them away later. Maybe when the urge struck to run the vacuum cleaner through the room. But for right now, I was going to have a look at Friday and Saturday's newspapers.

I thought I was. The minute I spotted the little diary on the cushion next to me, the newspapers got tossed back on the coffee table. What did Angel want from Joe? She knew he wasn't her father. Why had she gone to the trouble of writing a book of fiction? The answers refused to come, and I was going crazy trying to force them.

I went back over parts of my telephone conversation with Betsy. I was sure she hadn't mentioned what Angel went on to do once she was released from the detention center. She probably didn't know. Otherwise, she would have told me. Or else she didn't feel it was important enough stuff to pile on top of everything else. To me, every move that young woman made was important, especially now that I knew about the hideous things she was capable of doing.

She had gotten away with shutting her stepfather in that refrigerator, which resulted in his death. I could understand why she had done it, too. But why had she gagged and tied up Ethel in that refrigerator? Ethel was no threat to her. Or was she? Ethel wouldn't harm a fly, let alone a living soul. So she posed no physical threat to Angel. And the jealousy thing still didn't work for me. But she posed a threat to Angel in some way. Angel didn't just kill her for the fun of it. She had a reason. Just like she had a reason to try and set me up for the murder.

She didn't try, old gal, she did done it, that inner voice corrected.

This also reminded me my hours of freedom were coming to a rapid end. I had until Monday to prove my innocence; to prove Angel was the one the police really wanted. Even though they didn't know it yet.

FORTY-NINE

By the time the sun was supposed to be up, I had showered and dressed in a clean pair of jeans and sweatshirt. The rain had stopped, but the clouds held steady overhead, promising to dump more of their heavy load before moving on to torment elsewhere.

Kitty was waiting by her empty food dish when I entered the kitchen. I knew I couldn't get away with making a few telephone calls before tending to her need to be fed. So I opened a can of her food and spooned it into the dish before I picked up the phone.

As eager as I was to call Mitch, I made a quick call to Alicia's dormitory room first. I wasn't too disappointed when I pushed in the button to disconnect the ringing in my ear. Then I tapped in Mitch's numbers.

I was disappointed when his answering machine kicked on to the sound of his recorded voice. Just in case he hadn't left the farm yet, I left a message for him to call me, adding that it was urgent. If I was lucky, he'd return my call in the next few minutes. It was possible he was out in the barn feeding the assortment of farm animals he'd begun to accumulate over the past several months.

I waited around the house another twenty minutes or so for him to call. When he didn't, I grabbed the little diary off the couch and carried it with me into the garage and into the car. I drove past the church down the road from my place before I remembered it was Sunday. No point in going to Joe's place now. He'd be getting ready for early morning church service.

I spotted Mitch's pickup in the crowded parking lot outside the local gossip corner and pulled in and parked. As I went in the front door of the noisy restaurant, I saw the high school-aged girl behind the counter busy pouring coffee. Willie had Sundays off so she could attend church, too. And I hoped so she could get some rest after her six-day work week.

I headed toward the end booth after I got the young waitress's attention and gave her my breakfast order.

"Called your place earlier," I said as I slid in on the seat across from Mitch.

"Left early today," he informed as he folded up the newspaper he had been reading and put it down on the seat next to him.

"I got a call from Betsy during the night," I was telling him when the waitress arrived with my bowl of cold cereal and steaming coffee. She was thanked before she zipped off to tend to other customers who just came in the door.

I don't think Mitch even noticed I had chosen a healthier choice of food for breakfast. He was too eager for me to continue on with the details of my telephone conversation with Betsy. So I did. I relayed almost everything, word for word. I did leave off the beginning part about the unexpected passing of Betsy's mother-in-law.

When I finished, Mitch knew everything I knew about Angel Traditor's past. And once I had finished, he remained quiet for a while. I could tell he was worried. I also felt he wasn't talking yet because he needed the extra time for everything to sink in and settle first.

"Your friend Betsy's right, you know. None of this can be used against Angel. Can't even be reason to bring her in for questioning."

I ate my soggy cereal while Mitch did a little more thinking aloud. Basically, he was doing what I had done earlier by asking himself questions he seldom had answers for.

FIFTY

IT WAS MIDMORNING BY the time Mitch and I left the restaurant and went our separate ways. Mitch mentioned wanting to go visit with an old friend for a while, but he didn't say who. And I didn't press for a name.

I, on the other hand, told him I was going to pay Ethel's sister a visit. I still hadn't paid my respects to the family I had grown to know rather well over the years. There was another reason I wanted to see Edith. Perhaps she could shed some light on how Ethel had spent her last hours before she disappeared.

EDITH LIVED IN a big old house on Center Street. The house was well maintained over the years. The front and back yard were like one big flowerbed. Along the front porch tulips stood in full bloom and in a variety of colors. The flowers were the one bright spot in an otherwise dreary morning, I thought as I appreciated their beauty a few seconds more before going up the porch steps.

A multitude of food aromas drifted through the front screen door as I reached up and knocked. I tried to ignore the smells, and my stomach that gave out a hungry growl. The cereal just hadn't done the job it was supposed to do.

"What a pleasant surprise," Edith said with a smile as she crossed the front foyer headed in my direction.

"Morning, Edith," I said, and returned her pleasant smile with one I hoped didn't look forced.

"Well, come on in, girl."

I did. I stepped inside the house with its alluring odors that continued to torture me.

"I was just getting dinner 'round for the youngun's, you know. They'll be here soon as church lets out," said Edith, looking over her shoulder to make sure I was following her lead down the hallway and into the large kitchen. She tilted the lid on the large kettle that was about to boil over on the stove and turned back to me wiping her hands on her apron.

"Let's have us a little rest," she went on to say as she pulled out a table chair for me and another for herself.

I sat down and watched her shove aside plates that had been set at the places in front of us before she had a seat.

"So, how have you been, Fay? I didn't have a chance to talk with you at the cemetery yesterday." Her tone had softened with sadness by the time she finished that last sentence.

"I was shocked about Ethel."

"We were all shocked, girl. Terrible thing that was done to my sister. But I have faith the police will find the bad person who done it."

"So the police have talked to you, then?"

"Lordy, yes. Several times. They keep askin' the same questions. And I keep tellin' 'em the same answers. Guess they think I might remember something else each time they come back."

"What kind of questions do they ask?"

"You know, when the last time was I saw Ethel. If there was anybody new in her life she talked about."

"Was there?"

Edith jumped up and gave something on the stove a stir. Then she returned to her seat and finally answered me. "No one new that I know of. Last Sunday dinner was the last we seen our Ethel, you know."

I thought about bringing up Angel's name. To

hint about whether Ethel might have mentioned her. But I didn't have to. Edith did it for me.

"It's a blessin' the Lord sent Angel into Joe's life at this time."

"Isn't it, though" is all I could say.

"Such a sweet young thing. Joe told me all about things, you know, when he stopped by yesterday. Said Ethel knew all about the girl's mama. Angel must a been a big surprise to him, though."

"So what did Ethel think about Angel?"

"Don't know if Ethel got to meet Angel before... Well, you know what I mean.

"Suppose Angel could tell you if they ever got the chance to meet, though."

"Angel never said anything at the funeral about what a wonderful lady Ethel was? Or something that would make you think they had met?"

She looked off into space, as if she was giving it serious thought.

"No. She just said how sorry she was."

Edith's youngin's, as she put it, who are all of the adult age, and one my age, started filing into the house. I was invited to stay for dinner and accepted the invitation without hesitation.

FIFTY-ONE

IT WAS GOING ON TWO when I finally pulled myself away from the table at Edith's home. The one word that best describes my condition when I left was miserable.

The main course for dinner consisted of roast chicken, stuffing, mashed potatoes and gravy, and they weren't those instant potatoes either. An assortment of green and yellow vegetables was followed by dessert—homemade chocolate ice cream.

I had to slide my car seat back a notch in order to fit comfortably behind the steering wheel. But then, the word comfortable really wasn't appropriate. I doubted I'd be comfortable again for hours. And I probably wouldn't be ready to eat anything that carried any weight to it for at least a week.

The little book on the seat next to me reminded I couldn't go home and curl up on the couch for a nap as I would have liked to do. I had to see Joe.

I pulled into my usual spot behind Joe's big house

and crawled out from behind the wheel with more grunts and moans than I care to put a number to. If I would have thought to have a look through the garage window, I would have known nobody was home without traipsing up the backyard to the porch door.

The house was locked up tight. No evidence of life that I could tell. So I returned to my car and headed for home. It's only fair to say I was relieved Joe wasn't home. I was too full, and much too sleepy, to deal with the kind of emotional upheaval it would involve when I told Joe Angel was not his daughter.

KITTY DEMANDED another dish of food the minute I went in the door at home. As I spooned the fishy smelling stuff into her dish, I about lost my dinner on the spot.

"How can you eat this stinking crap?" I said, as she began lapping up the disgusting looking and smelly stuff. "You know, if you're not careful, you'll soon look as grotesque as I do," I informed her as a hand went to my swelled belly.

Again, before I headed into the living room to curl up on the couch, I told the fluffy feline where I'd be if she cared to join me. Twenty minutes tops,

I promised myself as I curled into a fetal ball. Then I'd be ready to start making telephone calls, one to Alicia and one to see if Joe made it home yet.

FIFTY-TWO

I THINK IT WAS THE sound of rain slashing against the house windows that drugged me into semi-consciousness. Or it could have been that eerie feeling I get when I sense I'm being observed closely that made me throw open my eyelids.

Kitty was sitting on the edge of the couch cushion staring at me. The second I reached up to touch her, she gave out one of her testy meows and jumped to the floor. "I didn't want to pet you anyway," I told her before the yawns and stretches came as I worked myself up into a sitting position.

It took a few seconds for my eyes to focus properly and to see darkness was falling around me. That put speed into me. I was on my feet in a flash when I saw the numbers the hands on the grandfather clock in the corner were pointed at. I had slept half the day away. Something a woman in my position could not afford to do. The hours of freedom were numbered for this old gal.

There wasn't time to waste making telephone calls. I didn't take precious seconds to check the answering machine for messages, either. If someone had called, surely I would have heard the ringing.

I was in my car and on the road in less than five minutes. I did give the parking lot at the local gossip corner a quick look as I sped by. I didn't think Mitch's pickup was there. But I certainly wouldn't swear to it.

This time when I parked behind Joe's place, I did have that quick look through the garage window. His Mercedes was parked inside. So I hurried up the backyard. I also remembered my umbrella, but the way the rain was coming down, I was getting hit from all sides anyway. I had Marie's diary shoved down the front of my jeans with my sweatshirt covering the top part that stuck out of my pants. So I was confident that little book was staying dry.

Joe saw me before I reached up and gave the screen door a rap. He was sitting at the kitchen table facing the door. I could see he had been reading something of importance. He had on his glasses.

"Come on in, Fay," he said, motioning me inside. Then he folded up his legal-sized papers and shoved them under the napkin holder that served as table centerpiece. He removed his reading glasses and carefully returned them to their case that stuck out of his dress shirt pocket.

I took a quick look around me before I joined him at the table. Angel was not within eyesight. This disturbed me as much as it pleased me.

"You just missed Allen and that friend of his, Dana."

"Allen was here?" I asked surprised, while I called my ex a liar inside my head. He told me it was over between him and the little beauty queen.

"He brought my new will by for signing. That Dana girl was a witness to my signature. She notarized the thing too. Hope you don't mind."

"Of course I don't mind," I was quick to respond. If she was here for a legal purpose, and not as Allen's girlfriend, what would be the point in getting all bent out of shape.

"Allen ain't such a bad fellow, I guess. He did say he wouldn't charge no extra for making a house call. Or because it was a Sunday. So I'd say there's some good left in him."

I had an idea Joe was headed somewhere with all this talk about Allen suddenly being one of the good guys again. I can't repeat the things he had said about him when he filed for divorce from me, which is why I was a little suspicious here.

"You want a read the thing?" Joe offered as he reached for the papers he had shoved under the napkin holder just a few minutes ago. "It's not the original. Just a copy. Allen's got the one that counts with him."

"It's really not my place to read your will, Joe," I told him when his fingers pushed the folded papers across the table toward me.

"You're in it, you know. Angel and you get it all." His voice had softened to almost a whisper when he next said, "Ethel's name was taken off this new one and Angel's put on in her place."

I wanted to ask where Angel was. But I couldn't speak. The adrenaline was torpedoing through the system too rapidly at that very moment for me to form words and then say them slow enough to be understood. I finally knew why Ethel had to die. All the more for Angel. If I were out of the way, the pie would be even bigger. Everything was beginning to make perfect sense. Angel wanted Joe for her papa because she wanted his money. Allen told me months ago Thomas was broke, on the verge of filing for bankruptcy. And Angel would know this. Or at least she had access to the information during those weeks she worked as a temp in Allen's law office.

I didn't know where to begin, but I had to tell Joe.

I had to warn him. Angel was an extremely dangerous woman. She was also a very smart one.

"Father, you should have told me we had
company again," Angel said as she entered the
kitchen from the hallway.

I swallowed long and hard before I dared look
up. I had to get myself ready for those doll-eyes of
hers. The ones that when you looked into them
deeply, you saw darkness, the emptiness—and pure
evil.

"If it wasn't getting so late, I'd offer you some
tea, Fay."

I had been told this as I watched her slither
around behind Joe and give his hunched over shoulders a rather rough looking squeeze. "Father here
really has had a very long day. I just came down to
help him along to bed."

My limbs were beginning to jerk from my indeci-
sion of what to do here. Do I spill the beans? Do I
tell Angel I know she's the one who murdered
Ethel? And that I know why now. Do I pull out
Marie's diary and hand it over to Joe while I tell him
Angel is not his daughter, but his brother,
Thomas's?

Before I made up my mind of what to do, Angel
was dropping pills into Joe's mouth and handing

him a glass of water to wash them down with. "Now you'll sleep like a baby," she told him sweetly, while her eyes glared at me destructively.

And that is the appropriate word, because any courage I had was falling away from me with the speed of lightning. I was trembling as I stood. I hoped my words were audible and without slur when I apologized for dropping by at such a late hour before making my abrupt departure.

FIFTY THREE

THUNDER ROARED FROM above and lightning flashed behind me as I ran for cover to my car. I let the wind have my umbrella before I dove into the front seat. I drove as if I had plans to outrun the lightning that was striking everything it could reach behind me.

Mitch flicked his lights at me and honked his horn before I realized it was him passing next to me. I slammed on my brakes while Mitch backed his pickup to my door. I hit my window button and watched him hand crank his down.

"I've been lookin' all over the place for you," he hollered over, squinting as the rain splashed against his face.

"I know why she did it," I hollered over his way.

"You mean Angel?"

I shook my head yes and hit the window button after yelling over for him to meet me at the local gossip corner.

WATER WAS RUNNING OFF both of us as we headed for our usual booth. A different waitress from earlier in the day arrived to take our orders. I ordered coffee, not so sure my stomach was ready for even that just yet. Mitch ordered the same.

The minute we were alone, I told Mitch about Joe's will. Angel was after his money. That's why the charade of who she really was. And that's why Ethel had to die. Angel wanted the money all to herself.

"Once I'm arrested for Ethel's murder, Joe will cut me out of the will too. Angel gets it all then."

"After Joe's gone?"

"Right. Oh, my God! Do you know what this means? Once I'm arrested and Joe eliminates me from his will—"

"Angel eliminates Joe," Mitch finished for me.

"What are we gonna do?"

"You're gonna go home" I was told by way of an order.

"What about you. Where are you going?"

"I'm goin' to talk to Lewis."

"So am I."

"No. If you go to him with this crazy story he'll think you're guilty for sure."

"Oh, I get it. Hearing it from you is gonna make it credible. Whereas—"

"Get over it, Fay. You're not goin' along."

We left our coffees at the booth without touching a drop. Mitch handed the waitress a couple of ones and didn't wait for change. Then we once again braved the raging thunderstorm outside. Mitch was going to see his lieutenant friend, and I was going home and locking myself inside until I heard from him.

FIFTY-FOUR

As I WAS BACKING OUT of the parking lot, I could have sworn my headlights passed over the back end of Joe's Mercedes parked at the edge of the restaurant.

"No, couldn't have been," I said, deciding the heavy rain and darkness made it near impossible to identify much of anything with complete accuracy, let alone the back of a car I barely got a glimpse of.

Mitch headed south and I headed east toward home. I had the wipers on high, but it was still difficult to see very well. So I kept my speed down.

It was less than a mile to the road I wanted to turn onto. I reached for my turn signal and glanced up in the rear-view mirror to make sure nothing was going to slam into the back of me when I slowed to a stop, while I waited for the eighteen-wheeler to pass next to me before I crossed over into his lane to make the turn off.

The second time I glanced up in the mirror, out

of the corner of my eye, I thought I saw something move in the backseat. This creepy sensation swept over me; then it struck again, only it tiptoed down inside of me and stayed there.

I wanted to look over my shoulder. No, that's incorrect. I thought I should look over my shoulder, but was momentarily too afraid. Once I made the turn, though, and had the wheel straightened out, I did start to look. I almost laughed too, for giving myself such a scare.

I was tilting my head around when, "Boo," shot up at me from behind.

I screamed and lost my grip on the wheel. The car swerved into the opposite lane. Luckily nothing was coming.

"Easy there, Fay," the haunting voice warned.

My fingers reconciled with the steering wheel and immediately stuck fast. The car was jerking because my right foot jumped on and off the gas pedal.

"Calm, Fay. We don't want a have us an accident on a night like this, now do we?"

I wasn't sure anything would come out when I attempted to speak, but I gave it a try anyway.

"What do you want, Angel?"

"Slow down, Fay. We don't want to miss your driveway either, now do we?"

I ordered my foot to ease off the accelerator so I could make the turn okay without knocking over my mailbox.

"Push the garage button, Fay," I was instructed as if I was a pre-school-aged child.

I wanted to scream, I don't need a lesson on how to get into my own garage. The only lesson I needed was a refresher course on why when we leave our vehicle we lock our doors.

There was a moment there, as I maneuvered the Lincoln into the garage, which is large enough to park two large cars, when I thought I might smash into the junk piled along the east wall. I reluctantly reached up to the visor and hit the button on the remote a second time to close the door. To lock the two of us inside. This was done because I didn't want to be given instructions again.

Then the car was shifted into park. The ignition turned off. And I was about to twist around in my seat to repeat my earlier question of what she wanted.

I wasn't given the chance. Something shot over my head and wrapped around my throat. I was being choked. On impulse, my hands flew to my throat to try and free myself.

"Let go, Fay, and I will."

I had to take her word for it she would keep her promise. Because if I didn't, I had a strong hunch she was going to win the struggle here. My fingers slid down to my chest, and Angel released the pressure. I coughed. And I coughed some more before I could finally breathe properly again.

Then I heard the door behind me open. I couldn't look around to see if Angel was stepping outside though. She still had what felt like a pair of panty hose wrapped around my neck, and drawn tight. At least I now understood why a man would complain about wearing a tie for any length of time.

Then I thought about Ethel. Is this how it happened with her?

Angel had stepped outside, because when I was ordered to get out of the car slowly, her voice came at me from the outside. And the panty hose had pulled slightly to the left and upward.

I worked my way out of the front seat. Then I gained knowledge of what a canine experiences as his master jerks him around by the choker chain.

FIFTY-FIVE

UNLOCKING THE DOOR so we could enter the house was not the typical routine task. But it was accomplished, and I was pulled and dragged around the kitchen before we ended up in the living room. In the process of getting there, I tried to keep from spilling the half full glass of water Angel handed me before we left the kitchen.

I started to ask her what the water was for, but my words were choked off in mid sentence.

"The couch is your favorite resting spot in the house. Isn't it, Fay?"

The noose around my neck loosened just enough for me to answer yes. My "Why," was cut off.

And if I could have, I would have ask how she knew where I liked to rest. But she was pulling on the panty hose again, moving me around to the front of the couch. The toe of my sneaker accidentally ran into the crutches I had propped along the one end of the couch. It was a reflex movement that had me reaching for them before they tipped over.

Angel got a hold of the crutches first though, and returned them to their upright position. Then she took the glass from me and put it down on the coffee table alongside newspapers.

"The water, Fay, is to help you swallow this bottle of sleeping pills." The ones she had pulled out of her rain coat pocket and dangled in front of me before placing them next to the water.

"Terrible thing what you went and done to Ethel. The wig is going to be the evidence that convicts you."

I tried to speak out in protest, but the panty hose tightened. My breath was being choked off again. "You'd rather kill yourself than spend the rest of your life locked away, Fay."

Her eyes were suddenly holding mine prisoner as she tightened the choke hold a little more. I don't know if it was because my face must have been changing colors from lack of oxygen to the brain, or if it was because she felt confident about who was in control here, that she loosened the hold.

I was still gulping in air when she informed me, "Your friend, Joe, decided to check out tonight as well.

"Maybe you'll see one another in hell, Fay."

My fear was swiftly replaced with anger. It seemed odd, but I think knowing Joe's hours were numbered is what was responsible for the anger more so than knowing my demise was upon me as well.

"No one will believe it." The hoarse voice that spoke was mine. "Two suicides on the same night—"

Another choke hold cut me off.

"Joe is devastated by the loss of Ethel. I will confirm it. He made out a new will so quickly so his daughter can buy the happiness he won't be around to provide."

My eyes told her happiness couldn't be bought. Then repeated the line that no one would believe the two suicides.

"You, Fay, have been miserable for a while now. Your husband doesn't want you anymore. Your daughter's off at college. You're all alone, Fay. Nobody wanted you anymore, except Joe. And with Ethel gone, you'd have him all to your depressing, fat self. You had to get rid of her.

"If it wasn't for that wig being found, you might have gotten away with it. But then there's the lipstick on Ethel's dress sleeve. It's the same shade you wear on occasion, Fay."

I had forgotten about the lipstick. My eyes told

her as much. They also asked a question she answered next, as if she really could see into my thoughts.

"I have been preparing for this for some time now, Fay. Ethel's murder was planned with you in mind to be accused." She loosened her grip on the panty hose. "Is there anything you'd like to say before you go to sleep, Fay? You know, any last words? But do be nice, Fay."

I had dozens of words, questions that still hadn't been answered. But there was one that came to mind first. "Why Joe, and not your real father?"

The choke hold was back, tighter than all the times before. Angel's eyes glared with anger, hate and outright evil. Then I watched her mouth move into this wicked sort of smile.

"Thomas was a fool not to acknowledge me. A mistake that cost him his life, you know."

So she had confronted him. And she also was responsible for his demise. Mitch was right from the very beginning; Thomas had had help sliding beneath the bath water.

"My daddy had a very bad cold. I watched him go to the doctor, to the drug store to fill his prescription for an antibiotic. I even watched him use the key he had hidden under the flower pot on his front porch. The medicine made him sleepy, Fay. He was asleep that night I tiptoed into his bathroom."

The noose around my neck was going limp as she proceeded with the story about how she murdered her biological father. "The man was old, out of shape, sick and asleep. So you see, Fay, it was easy to hold his head down."

"Oh, he struggled at first, but I jumped into the tub with him. Had my knees pressed into his chest and throat."

Her eyes glazed in another direction. It was as if she left the present and returned to the past when she said, "Just like that animal my mother married did to me."

Then she returned.

"It only took a few minutes. And how fortunate for me my knees left no marks. Or if they did, the coroner missed them."

My chance to attempt escape was now or never. Angel's story was coming to a close. I could feel it. I was sure when she was finished, I would be too.

One, two, three, and I lunged forward, only to be severely yanked back. This before she gave my stomach a hard shove, knocking me back onto the couch, also releasing the choke hold around my neck.

"What you got under there, Fay?" she demanded, as her eyes steadied on my stomach.

Marie's little diary had been down the front of my pants so long now that I had gotten used to the minor discomfort. Practically forgot the book was even there. But then I did have other things on my mind. When her hand headed in the direction of my waist, I made up my mind she wasn't going to touch me there. I hiked up my sweatshirt and pulled the little book out. My eyes asked her if she wanted the book a split second before I tossed it over the coffee table and in the direction of the unlighted fireplace.

When she lurched forward for it, in an attempt to grab it in midair, I moved in the opposite direction. I had the crutch in my hand and swung it up with all my might. I whacked her along the side of the head before she knew what hit her. Her head caught the corner of the coffee table on her way to the floor. After a few moments to level out my breathing, I quickly undid the panty hose from around my neck. Then I used the end of the crutch to poke Angel in the ribs. Not even a moan.

I grabbed the cordless phone off the end table and was thankful I only had to hit two numbers to reach Joe's place. And that was a chore in itself since my fingers, my whole body was shaking. I let it ring and ring. No answer.

The 911 I tapped in next was done feverishly.

The entire time my hoarse voice rapidly dictated instructions to the woman on the other end of the line, my eyes remained on the monster sprawled out on my living room floor. It seemed like an eternity before I was through giving addresses and situations for my place and Joe's.

I don't know why, but I took the necessary extra seconds to pick up Marie's diary, but didn't take a few more to check to see if Angel was still breathing.

Kitty suddenly decided to make her presence known as I crossed the kitchen and headed for the garage. I think I told her she'd have to wait for her dinner before I closed the garage door behind me.

FIFTY-SIX

I DROVE INTO THE LIGHTNING. If there was a buildup of carbon in my car's exhaust system, it got blown out the back.

I heard the scream of sirens and thought I was about to be pulled over for speeding on Broadway. I didn't slow down. And I didn't see any flashing red lights when I glanced up in the mirror.

When I turned onto Popular Avenue, I saw the sirens and flashing lights were coming from Joe's place.

"Boy, that was fast," I said in reference to my 911 call to send help. Realistically, I knew police and ambulance couldn't have arrived that quickly.

My speed increased before I jammed on the brakes. The car tires skidded against wet pavement, and stopped within inches of the Lincoln sideswiping the fire truck. An ambulance was backed up to the porch. And this old gal was out of her car and racing toward it without thought of the extended damage I put the ankle in jeopardy of sustaining. I felt no pain, only a sense of urgency to get to my dear friend, Joe Wise.

He was on a Gurney being wheeled out the door and up into the ambulance. His eyes were closed. An oxygen mask covered his nose and mouth. And I was frantically demanding to know from paramedic or attendant if he was going to be okay.

"Fay, he's gonna be okay," the voice that belonged to the pair of hands that landed on my shoulders assured.

Mitch guided me out of the way. But my eyes followed Joe, and remained on him until the ambulance door was pushed shut.

"If it wouldn't a been for Mitch here, it might a been all over for that old guy, though." I looked up into the face that went with the deep male voice.

Lieutenant Lewis Evans towered next to Mitch. He was looking down at me.

"Angel did it," I shouted, hoping to be heard over the sudden squeal of the siren behind me as the ambulance started to pull away.

"Mitch told me the story. That's why we were here. Come to have us a chat with this Angel woman."

"She isn't here, Fay," Mitch was quick to jump in and tell me.

"No kidding. She was out cold on my living room floor when I left home."

"You say she's in your house?" This came from the lieutenant. Mitch looked too surprised to speak.

"I clobbered her across the head with my crutch. She was trying to force me to swallow a bottle of sleeping pills. It was supposed to be a suicide. The same with Joe."

"Like I said, if it weren't for Mitch here, Mr. Wise would have inhaled enough gas to put him to sleep for good."

"Gas?"

"Good I quit smokin' when I did." Mitch finally had found his voice.

"Otherwise, I never would a been able to smell it."

I think it was the confused look I was giving him that made him clear things up for me.

"When Lewis and me got here, the house was dark. Everything locked up tight. My taste buds and smeller started workin' again a few weeks after I quit those cancer sticks. Anyway, we're walkin' 'round the house, tryin' doors and stuff, and I smell gas."

"The gas on the old kitchen stove was turned on full blast. Light a match in there and the whole place would a blown," the lieutenant informed.

I finally looked around and saw windows pushed up. I also heard the lieutenant ask a borough police officer to get on his radio and send the troops to my place, pronto.

FIFTY-SEVEN

I WANTED TO FOLLOW the ambulance to the hospital so I could be with Joe. But I decided I'd feel safer once I watched handcuffs slapped on Angel. Then I could follow her to the hospital so her head injuries could be tended to before she was hauled off to jail.

Mitch trailed me home, where my driveway was lit up with flashing lights that sat atop at least a half dozen police cars. Luckily, the rain wasn't coming down by the bucketful anymore, since I had to park at the edge of the driveway.

I heard Mitch start to tell the state trooper that stopped us before our feet landed on the driveway who we were. But I didn't hear his last words. I took off running for the house when I spotted Alicia standing near my wide open front door.

"Mom," exclaimed Alicia the instant I charged through the doorway. I wanted to grab her and shake her one for what she had done. I also wanted to throw my arms around her and tell her how glad I was she had come home. And that's what I did.

"Mom, are you all right?" she asked, as she wiggled herself out of my bear hug-type embrace.

"I'm fine, honey," I told her, while my eyes began searching for Angel. When I saw only police officers examining the area in front of the living room fireplace, I demanded from whoever, "Where is she?" I noticed the blood droppings on the carpet that led from the living room, into the foyer, and out the front door, before my question was finally answered.

"The woman that everyone around here's been looking for, isn't here, Mom. I told them that. When I got here, the front door was hanging open."

"Sorry again, Miss, for the misunderstanding," the handsome young state trooper was suddenly saying to Alicia. I was taken back a bit when I saw the way the two of them were looking at each other. I recognized the look. And the thought that crossed my mind was, Heaven help us, she's turning into her father.

She supposedly got hitched yesterday or today, and already is looking at this handsome young man as if it were love at first sight.

"Alicia?"

It took a tug on her arm before she blinked and gave me a small fraction of her attention.

"At first, Brian thought I was the woman they were looking for."

"Brian, huh? How wonderful" is all I could say at the moment.

"They said she's gone, Fay," Mitch said, as he walked up next to me. "I know. But she can't have gone far. She's hurt. And she's on foot."

"Right. But the interstate's not even a half mile away. She could a hitched a ride and be long gone by now."

I had my doubts about that. And I told Mitch as much. What suddenly occurred to me next sent panic into me.

"Joe! What if she finds out he's been taken to the hospital? What if she goes there to finish—"

"Already taken care of. A guard's bein' put on Joe as we speak. A few plain-clothed guys are headed over there too. So you can relax."

"I won't be able to do that until that awful woman is in custody."

"I see another young lady decided to come home."

My daughter had Brian backed against a wall. They were smiling at each other. I'm not sure which one of the two was putting the moves on the other. I did know one of those mother-daughter talks was way overdue.

FIFTY-EIGHT

IT TOOK ANOTHER HOUR before the invasion on my home ended. Everyone had gone, including Mitch. He planned to join forces with the troops who planned to comb the surrounding area outside for Angel.

The house was sealed up as tight as a drum before Mitch departed, though. And he had done so with the promise to call me the minute Angel was captured.

Because I was more or less ordered to remain behind locked doors, I didn't drive to the hospital to check on Joe. But I did call. I was told his condition had stabilized. He'd probably sleep the night away. I was told not to bother driving over; he wouldn't know I was there anyway. Best to wait until morning when, I was assured, he'd be awake and alert.

I put down the receiver and turned to face my daughter, who was sitting at the kitchen table spooning the marshmallows off the top of her cup of hot chocolate. She looked up long enough for our eyes to have a brief meeting.

Then, "Can't it wait till morning, Mom? I'm exhausted."

"Do you have any idea what you put your father and I through this weekend, young lady?

"My God, I forgot to call your father."

"He already knows I'm home. I called him before you got here. And if it will make you feel better too, I didn't go through with it," she tacked on at the end.

I pulled a chair out from the table and dropped into it.

"You okay?"

A heavy sigh was followed with, "I will be."

"Do you want to talk about it?"

"Yeah. But not right now." Allen's eyes looked over at me, but the face was mine. "You don't mind if I crash here tonight and head back to school in the morning, do you?"

"It will be nice having you here. Especially after the kind of day I had."

"Pretty crazy, huh?"

"I could think of a few other words, but I guess I'll settle for crazy." We smiled together.

Then we went up to bed together. Alicia headed

straight to her room after saying goodnight at the top of the stairs.

I wasn't ready for sleep. I did have that super long nap earlier, after all. And I also had this uneasy feeling floating around inside of me. I knew it would remain with me until Angel was apprehended by the police.

Hopefully, that would happen before the night was over. If not, I just may have to consider what Mitch had said as a real possibility. There is a truck stop nearby. The place had the works—restaurant, shower, movie and video areas and fuel station. A hop, skip and jump from the place was the interstate. If Angel knew the police were after her, she may just have decided to hitch a ride with one of the truckers, and be in another state by daybreak.

I kicked off my sneakers and stretched out on the bed on my back. I decided I'd close my eyes and try to at least rest for a little while. Try to clear some of the clutter from the head in the process.

That's what I did, too. I concentrated deeply on cleansing the head. Moving to a place of tranquility. I was almost there, drifting into this calm, peaceful cloud of fluff.

Then the black curtain came down. On top of me. I couldn't breathe. I threw open the eyelids to see total darkness and feel the powerful pressure on my face. On top of me. My arms and legs thrashed about, smacking into the stiff form bearing down on my chest. I was losing the struggle with the bed pillow that was smothering me, and the form atop me.

In my struggle, I managed to turn my head slightly to the side, so I breathed in enough air to last me a few seconds longer. I used those seconds to go limp. Play dead. And I was headed in that direction, about to lose consciousness when the pressure on my face began to ease.

In no way did I believe I had the strength to get up, much less throw the weight from my chest. But that inner voice ordered me to do it. And the adrenaline gushed from the brain to parts of the body where needed, because when I reached up and latched onto bony arms, superwoman took over.

I rolled to my side, throwing Angel off me and onto the floor. As I sprang off the bed and headed for the door, she jumped on my back, her fingers pulling hair and digging into neck flesh. But I didn't give in to the scratches and hair pulls from the wild creature riding me. I swung around and smashed her into a dresser.

She howled in pain when the dresser's pointed knobs poked into her spine. But she held on. And held on some more until I started to weaken. I dropped to my knees. But when I tucked my right shoulder under and rolled, I brought my knee up and clipped her a direct shot to the nose.

That got her to let go of me and pull back. And gave me enough time to make it out into the hall. Just in time to see a sleepy-eyed Alicia open her bedroom door and groan, "What's all the commotion?" I saw Alicia's eyes and mouth open wide as she looked over my shoulder.

"Lock your door and call the police," I screamed at her as I took a look over my shoulder.

Angel was coming for me again. Blood ran from her nose. There was some crusted blood against the blonde hair near her temple that gaped open from the wound she received in our earlier tussle.

Alicia never was one to be ordered around, and was coming to assist me, instead of locking herself in her room.

But it wasn't Alicia who saved me from another brutal attack. Angel's feet got tangled up in Kitty near the top of the stairs. Kitty hissed and swatted at Angel's legs to free herself. In the brief exchange, I watched Angel lose her balance and dive over the banister.

I squeezed my eyes shut with the sound of the

hard thud from below. Alicia's hands held in her scream of horror. My daughter finally listened to my order for her not to look. And to the next one for her to go call the police.

After I watched her disappear into her bedroom, I peeked over the banister.

Angel had landed face up. Her right leg was bent back under her left knee joint. Inner arms were stretched out facing me. And doll-eyes glared straight up at me.

I knew she was dead.

Kitty beat me to the bottom of the stairs. She made one cocky prance around Angel. Then she hissed and growled before flying back up the stairs.

I didn't prance around the dead body. I did not feel proud. My own body was still experiencing aftershock tremors. When I slowly bent down and reached over to close Angel's eyes, I saw her blonde hair had shifted backward on the top of her head. In front, short dark hair was flattened to her scalp. The blonde hair was a wig. Angel was a brunette.

Sirens began surrounding the house and I straightened back up. As I did so, I reminded myself there was a lesson to be learned here. My blonde-bashing days were over. A brunette can be a dangerous woman too.

Or how about a redhead?

FIFTY-NINE

I WAS AT JOE'S BEDSIDE by the time the sun came up Monday morning. And I kid you not, the sun was up, throwing its brilliant rays as far as I could see.

There were tears shed between Joe and I when I told him the necessary details of the previous night. The gaps in the story were filled in with the horrendous events that led up to Angel's tragic end.

A few smiles were shared too, in appreciation for surviving Angel's lethal plans for the two of us. We agreed that the lives that had been lost were senseless, Angel's included. Although I know I will sleep a lot better knowing that woman will never be a threat to another living soul. I don't know about the dead ones, though.

I left Marie's diary with Joe. And he held it against his heart as we exchanged good-byes for the day.

MITCH ARRIVED AT the local gossip corner as I was getting out of my car.

"A little late for you to be arriving for breakfast, isn't it?" I asked with a smile from where I had waited at the restaurant door for him.

"If a certain woman wouldn't keep me up all hours of the night." His comment was followed by a smile before we headed inside to our usual rear booth.

Over a hearty breakfast, we decided that Angel had to have been in my house the entire time the police carried out their massive search outdoors. Mitch then happened to mention the police were producing enough evidence on Angel that I should be cleared from the pending charge of murder by the end of the week.

I certainly hoped so.

BEFORE I LEFT the house Monday morning, I gave Doug a call at his home. He was informed the ankle had mended sufficiently enough for me to deliver papers that day. I decided not to ruin his day by telling him I decided to keep my newspaper business after all. I'd save that news for another day. One when he published something that spoiled my day.

All in all, Monday was a good day. Correction, it was a *great* day. My daughter was still single and on her way back to college. Joe had survived the attempt on his life. And I had survived, too.

Yes, I was extremely grateful to be outside in the refreshing afternoon sunshine, tossing rolled newspapers onto porches again. Freshly washed laundry danced in the wind from the lines it hung from, making me feel like doing a jig or two myself.

As I headed up the Fergusons' front porch, I reached into my shoulder bag for something other than a newspaper. A dog biscuit was slipped inside the screen door before the newspaper. And as a result, I had gained a feisty little terrier for a friend.

The big black tomcat that prowls outside the video store on the corner of Front Street and Broadway, greeted me with a pleasant meow as I passed by.

"M-e-o-w," I greeted right back.